"Kate, are you all right?" Max ran to where she was lying facedown in the sand.

She lay very still, wondering if it was too late to escape the powerful, handsome man she wanted much too much already.

Max turned her over and saw she was breathing. "Open you eyes, Kate." When she didn't respond, he muttered aloud, "Okay, I'll have to do CPR."

Kate's eyes flew open. "I'm fine. It's not necessary," she whispered.

"Better check your pulse," he said, pretending to look for the pulse point in her neck. His technique felt more like a caress, and Kate held her breath. "A bit rapid, I think. Better check the heartbeat." He laid his head across he breast and listened.

If her pulse had been erratic before, now it was playing pinball. "Get off me, Max! Are you trying to smother me?"

He began to laugh. "I guess I won't get to perform artificial respiration this time," he said with regret.

Kate rose from the sand, pulled off her top and shorts, and raced for the water. Max took off after her, and caught up just as a wave soaked them both. "Come here, you almond-eyed nymph from the sea," he said, pulling her to him. "We'd better get some sunscreen on you before you burn."

"Too late," Kate murmured as his lips nibbled at her shoulder. "We're already on fire. . . ."

WHAT ARE *LOVESWEPT* ROMANCES?

They are stories of true romance and touching emotion. We believe those two very important ingredients are constants in our highly sensual and very believable stories in the *LOVESWEPT* line. Our goal is to give you, the reader, stories of consistently high quality that may sometimes make you laugh, sometimes make you cry, but are always fresh and creative and contain many delightful surprises within their pages.

Most romance fans read an enormous number of books. Those they truly love, they keep. Others may be traded with friends and soon forgotten. We hope that each *LOVESWEPT* romance will be a treasure—a "keeper." We will always try to publish

LOVE STORIES YOU'LL NEVER FORGET
BY AUTHORS YOU'LL ALWAYS REMEMBER

The Editors

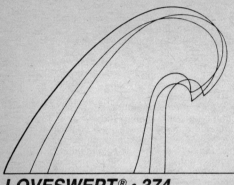

LOVESWEPT® • 374

Sandra Chastain
Penthouse Suite

BANTAM BOOKS
NEW YORK · TORONTO · LONDON · SYDNEY · AUCKLAND

PENTHOUSE SUITE

A Bantam Book / January 1990

If you would be interested in receiving protective vinyl
covers for your Loveswept books, please write to this address
for information:

Loveswept
Bantam Books
P.O. Box 985
Hicksville, NY 11802

ISBN 0-553-44005-5

Published simultaneously in the United States and Canada

Bantam Books are published by Bantam Books, a division
of Bantam Doubleday Dell Publishing Group, Inc. Its trade-
mark, consisting of the words "Bantam Books" and the
portrayal of a rooster, is Registered in U.S. Patent and
Trademark Office and in other countries. Marca Registrada.
Bantam Books, 666 Fifth Avenue, New York, New York 10103.

PRINTED IN THE UNITED STATES OF AMERICA

O   0 9 8 7 6 5 4 3 2 1

For Judy,
who believed in me from the start

One
___

A room and two weeks with pay in the ritziest place she'd ever worked! This was going to be a grand adventure, Kate Weston thought, as she hitched up her coveralls, pushed the cart containing her tool chest and supplies off the elevator, and knocked on the penthouse door.

No answer. She rang the doorbell.

"Maintenance," she called out, wondering if she'd misunderstood the manager's instructions to check the shower in the penthouse. Max Sorrenson, the hotel owner and the reclusive occupant of the penthouse suite, had called the maintenance department and requested that someone repair his shower. Why wasn't he answering the door? Maybe she was expected to use her pass key and go in.

Kate debated for a moment. She'd replaced a few light bulbs, but this was her first call as a member of the maintenance staff of La Casa del Sol. Did she dare? Of course. She opened the door and stepped inside, stopping her cart just in time to avoid a direct collision with a nearly nude man who gave new meaning to the word spectacular.

Shocked speechless, Kate could do nothing but stare. He'd obviously just stepped out of the shower. He wore a towel around his hips and had another one thrown over his head. He was leaning forward slightly, drying his hair briskly.

"My shower is leaking again."

His shower?

It wasn't that Kate had never seen a half-naked man up close. She had. It wasn't that Kate was inexperienced in dealing with men. She had often been the only woman on a work crew. It wasn't that Kate was normally tongue-tied. She hadn't ever been—until now.

But this particular man seemed to play havoc with her senses. His body was sun-kissed to the color of warm honey. Droplets of water beaded and rolled down his bare chest like arrows, drawing her attention to the loosely draped towel below.

Max Sorrenson was tall, but not too tall. He was solid and lean and emanated power. She compared him to Mr. September on the Chippendale calendar—and he didn't come up lacking!

Nah, she decided. The owner of the hotel couldn't be as young as his body appeared. Beneath the towel he was probably a Cesar Romero look alike. "Shades of *Falcon Crest*," Kate mumbled under her breath. From the time she'd walked into the Spanish hacienda-style hotel two hours earlier, she'd felt as if she were in the Tuscany Valley instead of on the Gulf Coast of Florida.

What she was gazing at was pure unadulterated, unrestrained male. The man definitely had a bad boy look that sent shivers right up her spine.

"The leak drips hot water on my feet, and by the time I'm halfway through a shower, the water has turned to ice," Max Sorrenson said as he twisted around and moved back toward the open bedroom door without stopping his hair-drying.

Even his voice was provocative. It was a deep, warm voice that belonged to a man who'd been born in the South and spent years away from the area. Kate tried to envision his body covered with a tan raincoat. Her ploy failed. Instead she envisioned him as Humphrey Bogart saying, "Here's looking at you, kid."

"Fix the shower, will you?"

He'd made his request a command, and Kate knew that she'd better get cracking. She cleared her throat. Ice water had he said? That was exactly what she needed, buckets full of the stuff to sink her head in. She was a maintenance engineer, not some awkward kid ogling a naked man.

Kate forced herself to look past the half-nude man to the bathroom. She pushed the cart inside and shook her head in astonishment. It wasn't a bathroom, it was a mini-ballroom, complete with mirrored walls and spotlights. Not only did the self-assured executive who'd met her at the door reek of sexuality, he created the proper setting for it. All he needed was Sophia Loren and a tub full of bubbles.

If Kate hadn't been dumbstruck first by the sight of the man, and second by the suite, she might have told him right away that she was filling in for Joe, who was in the hospital for two weeks. If he'd bothered to glance in her direction, he'd have known that she was a woman. Well, maybe. There hadn't been a mirror in the maintenance room, and until now she hadn't realized how scruffy she looked. She'd rolled up the cuffs of Joe's coveralls three times, and the garment hung from her body like some great orange pillowcase with seams. The only part of the uniform that fit was the matching orange cap she'd found hanging by the clothes rack.

Gamely, she opened her tool chest and attacked the plumbing problem. She suspected that the leak might be solved with a simple washer. Thank goodness for night school and the six years of how-to classes she'd worked her way through, she thought as she worked. Plumbing had been one of her best subjects.

Kate felt absurdly nervous as she tested the connections. The fixtures were old, not the washerless modern kind. She forced her attention to the pipes, applied the wrench, and tried to tighten the nut gently. The procedure might have worked if she hadn't glanced into the mirror at that moment and caught sight of Max Sorrenson just as he removed the towel from his head.

She'd been wrong. The man beneath the terry cloth wasn't older than thirty-five. Max didn't resemble the well-preserved Cesar Romero at all. It was the young hunk Lorenzo Lamas who paled in comparison. Max's hair was so dark and thick and glossy, a woman couldn't help but want to run her fingers through it. He had a strong face with winglike brows that capped incredibly dark eyes and lashes.

Kate, wrench in hand, froze as she noticed that the angle of the mirrored wall gave her a front row seat for the scene being acted out behind her. She knew she ought to call out, warn him to close the door, but thought better of drawing attention to the fact that she was staring. The man was so self-absorbed that he either didn't know or didn't care that she was watching. She'd been told how aloof he was. Maybe he thought of his employees as simply part of the furniture. She decided to get on with her work and try to ignore him.

But she couldn't resist watching as he dried his chest and his arms, shrugged his shoulders, and pitched the damp towel behind him. He opened two folding doors and stood in the middle of a walk-in closet, surveying the racks of clothing inside. Good, she thought, he'd soon be out of her line of vision. And then Mr. September loosened the towel from around his hips and let it drop.

Kate's gasp echoed through the silence like the explosion of a cannon. The wrench slipped, the pipe twisted, and a stream of cold water shot across the bathroom.

"What the—?" Max Sorrenson whirled around.

The stream of water slammed into Kate, shooting her cap into the mirrored wall, releasing her mass of dark hair. She dropped to the floor and began scrambling wildly for her tools.

"Who are you?" Max stared at the figure in the orange uniform in astonishment as he grabbed his towel and wrapped it around his waist.

"I said," he repeated, making no attempt to mask his growing anger, "who are you?"

"I'm Kate Weston."

"Just what do you think you're doing?"

Watching you, she almost said as she located her wrench and began to work at the pipe. She'd blown it now. From the expression on her employer's face she was going to be fired. There was no point in making small talk when they were about to be washed away. She didn't have time for polite conversation.

"I'm fixing a leak, Max. Put your pants on and hold this."

Max stared at the woman in total disbelief. The water abruptly ceased erupting and trickled to a stop. She motioned for him to take hold of her wrench. She was soaking wet, this waiflike woman who was wearing a hotel uniform with the name "Joe" plainly embroidered on the pocket just over her right breast. Breast? The uniform clung to her body like a wet T-shirt. Her breasts were small but full, he noted, with large areolas circling nipples peaked hard from being pelted by the icy water. For a long instant he could only stare at her.

She glared at him. "Hurry up, Max. I need to get this water cleaned up before it leaks into the room below."

"Then call a plumber," he said in a voice that sounded as remote as if it came from outer space.

"I am a plumber," she said with a bright smile. "And I don't think either one of us wants to call the desk for help right now, do we?"

Max followed her gaze from the floor to his slipping towel, and he took a deep breath. "No, that would not be a good idea."

Kate lifted her gaze to his face, determined not to let this penthouse tyrant put all the blame on her. If he hadn't dropped his towel in the first place, none of this would have happened. She stared at his frown, trying desperately not to let herself gawk at the towel.

So much for determination. She was weak. Lordy, she was ogling the man again, and he was standing there with a stunned expression on his face. As she watched, the stern expression died, humor welled up in his dark eyes, and the corners of his mouth began to curl.

Good, she thought, the man was human. It just took him a while to thaw out. It was her turn. She inclined her head and widened her eyes into what she hoped was an I-dare-you expression.

Max struggled to control the urge he had to let his towel drop. He forgot about the water sloshing over his feet. The woman wasn't backing down. She was bravely standing up to him, knowing that he held the power to dismiss her in an instant. The overhead lights bounced off the mirror and ricocheted a sparkle of silver across the beads of water that frosted her dark hair.

Call for help? He glanced into the mirror and blanched at the reflection of himself standing there grinning like an idiot. He was the one who needed help. But Max Sorrenson had never asked for help in his life. Analyze the problem and reach a proper solution, that was his method of approach.

"I guess you're right. What do you want me to do?"

"Well," she said quickly before she gave in to the urge to cover the distance between them and rip that scrap of cloth away. "I'd prefer that you got dressed first—that towel has already caused enough chaos—but there isn't time." Kate took a deep, calming breath, stepped to the side, and leaned out of the way so that Max could move close enough to take the wrench.

"I don't believe this is happening. This is a luxury hotel. We never have problems. I don't allow them." Max stepped into the bathroom and took hold where she indicated. "Are you new?"

"I'm filling in for Joe. He's in the hospital." Kate

selected the correct size washer from her cart. "I've got it. You can let go. I can stop the leak."

Max stepped aside and glared at the woman. "Forget the leak," he managed to say between clenched teeth, "just mop up this mess."

"I'll have to order another shower head," Kate said, trying to ignore the return of anger she read in her employer's face. She had the feeling that he was as confused over what had just happened as she. But she didn't want to test his control any further. John Wayne always outbluffed the bad guys. Maybe she could too. "This one is just worn out."

"Never mind the shower."

"Whatever you say," Kate began. "Look, I'm sorry about the flood. But if you hadn't taken my mind off what I was doing, it wouldn't have happened. I mean, Humphrey Bogart wouldn't have done that. I seriously doubt if Cesar Romero would have either." She knew she was talking nonsense, but she couldn't seem to stop herself.

Max shook his head, swallowed his words, whirled around, and left the bathroom. He stepped inside the walk-in closet and slammed the doors behind him. He threw a pair of shoes on the floor, grabbed clean underwear and a shirt. He reached toward the racks and pulled out the first pair of pants he touched. In less than a minute, he was dressed and balancing himself against the wall as he jammed his feet into his shoes.

Max opened the door and strode back to the bathroom, prepared to give a thorough tongue-lashing to the woman who'd done more to unsettle his psyche than anybody he'd ever met.

This time it was Max Sorrenson who swallowed hard and came to a screeching halt. The woman had unzipped the coveralls and was leaning over, drying her dark hair. The garment hung open, revealing the soft curve of her breasts. The uniform was pulled tight across her bottom, and he could see that she wasn't as thin as he'd first thought. Secretly leering at an employee was totally out of character for him. He'd never paid much attention to them one way or another—until now.

At that moment she straightened up, wiped the water from her face, and caught sight of Max behind her. He heard her sharp intake of breath, and for a moment she froze.

"Oh, I'm sorry. I just thought I'd dry myself off so that I wouldn't drip on your carpet."

She was taller than he'd thought too. Her hair was a rich dark brown, all tousled into a fine silken web. There was a streak of grease across one flushed cheek, and her lips parted uncertainly as she raised her gaze to meet his. "I am sorry."

"What for? I think that's a good idea." What was he saying? She had him muttering inane niceties when what he wanted to do was jerk her against him and kiss her senseless. He was even more astounded by the words he spoke next. "Why don't you borrow one of my robes and let me drop that uniform in the dryer?"

Take off her clothes? "Eh, no, thanks. I don't think so. I'll just jump on the elevator and get back to the maintenance department. I'll get dry clothes down there." What was she thinking? The man was only protecting the image of his hotel. He wasn't propositioning her. She was simply overreacting. Wasn't she?

Max watched her expression change. He'd never

seen such an expressive face. Sensing her tension, Max decided that the possibility of being fired was worrying her. He'd put her at ease by letting her know that he was simply being practical.

"And let the guests see one of my staff members looking like a refugee from the chain gang? Just wait in there, and I'll have someone bring up a dry uniform for you." That was being practical, wasn't it? he asked himself. Hell no, that was being brusque, the way he always reacted when he was threatened or unsure of himself.

Max stepped to the phone and punched a number. "Send one of the maids up here with a fresh pair of coveralls for the woman who's filling in for Joe."

Kate, glad to have his attention diverted from her, gathered up her tools, replaced them in the tool chest, and mopped the last of the water from the floor with the towel she'd used on her hair.

"Mr. Sorrenson, I want you to know that I don't normally make such a mess. I knew that a job in a place like this would be a grand adventure, but I never expected to sabotage my employer's home."

"Working as a plumber is a grand adventure?"

Her voice wasn't Dixie-soft and gentle like the women's voices he was accustomed to hearing. Rather, she had a funny hesitant, disjointed way of speaking, like an excited little girl at an amusement park. Curiosity, tension, wonder, excitement, one emotion followed the other across her face like the credits rolling at the end of a movie. "I don't believe that I ever knew anyone who thought plumbing was an adventure."

"I really didn't plan any of this. I wouldn't even be here if it weren't for the poodle and the lady in the wheelchair. Of course, it was really my car that caused the problem. It died in your driveway. Then she offered to have it repaired. Of course, I couldn't let her do that. Saving her life wasn't that big a deal. So I agreed to take Joe's place for two weeks while I get it running again. That's a fair exchange, don't you think?"

Lady in a wheelchair? This was beginning to make sense. At least the wild story he was hearing and its connection with the lady in the wheelchair was no surprise. He'd spent most of his life trying to make sense out of incidents that were more unbelievable. The lady in the wheelchair had to be his Aunt Dorothea, the woman who'd raised him. After almost thirty-six years, both of them had given up on ever understanding what made the other one tick.

"Ms. . . . what did you say your name was again?"

"Kate, Kate Weston."

"Miss Weston, I don't have any idea what you're talking about. But now that I know your presence here involves Dorothea Jarrett, it begins to make more sense. Before I do something rash, I think I'd better hear this story."

"Mrs. Jarrett. Yes, that's her name—the woman in the wheelchair. Do you know her?"

The doorbell pealed.

"Just hold on a minute. This ought to be your dry clothes." Max went to the door, opened it, and took the dry coveralls, closing the door firmly in the face of the young hotel employee.

Max looked down at the oversized garment he was holding and shook his head. "Don't we have any uniforms in a smaller size?" He handed the clothing to Kate and turned his back. "Get dressed, and then we'll talk."

Max smiled as he realized that from where he

was standing he could see the woman changing clothes behind him in his mirrored dressing room door. He couldn't resist taking a peek. He was right. Her legs were long. And she was thin, but not too thin. Her breasts were . . . just perfect.

A gentleman wouldn't have watched, he thought as he turned his head. But then a lady wouldn't have watched him earlier. As Dorothea always said, turnabout is fair play. But all he could think of was that it was a good thing he wasn't holding a wrench, or the entire suite would have been ankle-deep in water.

"Now, Kate. Start at the beginning."

They were sitting at the glass and chrome table in the kitchen. Max was drinking mineral water, and Kate was sipping from a can of cola.

"Are you sure this is all right? I mean, I should get back downstairs, shouldn't I?"

"Don't you have your pager?"

"Yes, sir. It's on my cart."

Sir? Now that she wasn't being threatened, his wild woman with the wrench had suddenly become the uncertain employee. "They know where you are. They'll page you if you're needed. I'm waiting to hear how you came to take Joe's place."

"Well, here goes. I guess it started when I got my last paycheck. I mean, it wasn't my boss's fault. He was a nice old man who owned a television repair business. He couldn't pay me much, but he let me live in the shop. Business wasn't very good. Then he lost his lease, and my last check bounced. He needed the money more than I did. Otherwise I would have installed a new water pump in my car before I left. I'd already been in

Atlanta for three months, and Florida was next on my list. I just took a chance."

"Do you always take chances?"

Her hair was dry now. It curled softly across her shoulders. Her square-shaped face, bare of any makeup, seemed determined and proud. There was a tiny scar over her upper lip, and he wondered how she'd gotten it. There was something free and natural about the woman that Max couldn't quite pin down.

"Take chances? Me? Sure, all the time. Don't you?"

"No. Well, I suppose I do to some extent when I'm playing the market. But even then I never make a move unless I've studied all the possibilities carefully."

"Market? As in stocks?" In her mind, the man across the table changed into the stern, manipulative, cold stockbroker Michael Douglas played in *Wall Street*. And then Max smiled. "Is that how you made all your money?" she asked.

"No. I inherited a fishing fleet. And I've managed to make a few wise investments."

"Must be nice. I've never worked for anybody who was rich. Well, except for Lolly Daye, the owner of Lolly's Amusement Park in Tennessee, but I never actually met her."

"Were you a plumber there?"

"No. I was a painter. I worked on the carousel. The animals were magical. There was one special one, a unicorn. He was all white and gold. I could sit on his back, close my eyes, and imagine I was anywhere."

Carousel. Max had a flashing memory of the first time he'd ever seen the carousel on the Carnival Strip. He'd been just a child. The animals had seemed gigantic to him on the first ride, and he'd held on to his horse's reins for dear life. Dorothea had been on the giraffe next to him, pretending to be a cowgirl and yahooing at the top of her lungs. He hadn't thought of that carousel in years.

"What brought you to my hotel?"

"Oh, I never intended to stay here permanently. I knew this place was too rich for my blood. But La Casa del Sol, a place in the sun—I couldn't resist staying one night. Then came the poodle and the wheelchair, and my car died. It was fate."

Max took a swallow of mineral water and wondered what he was doing sharing his kitchen with a woman who lived in a TV repair shop, painted carousels, and repaired her own car. He'd never met a woman who moved from place to place.

"I never knew women moved around like that, unless they were circus employees or migrant workers. I thought all women wanted to settle down. You know, roots, that sort of thing."

"Not me. Not yet. Maybe someday, after I've been everywhere and done everything. For now, my plan is to do something different every day for the rest of my life. Roots? That's just another name for chains. And that's one thing I'm not interested in. After three months in one place, I'm out. What about you? What do you do for fun?"

"Me? I don't know. I don't suppose I ever thought much about it before. I've always had goals and worked to reach them. That gives me great pleasure."

"You mean making money?"

"Yes, I guess it does boil down to that. Goals, problems, solutions, success. Fun never entered into it."

"Sounds dull to me. How old are you, Max?"

"I'll be thirty-six on my next birthday. How old are you, Kate?"

"I'll be twenty-six on my next birthday. At first I thought you were older. More like Cesar than Lorenzo."

Max wasn't certain he liked being thought of as old. "Cesar and Lorenzo? Who are they?" he asked curiously. The woman kept him constantly off balance.

"They star in a Friday night television series called *Falcon Crest*. Cesar Romero is the suave older wealthy lover. Lorenzo Lamas is the young rich stud."

"I take it you're making a comparison to my wealth rather than to my sexual prowess."

Max tilted his head quizzically and gave Kate a smile that made her feel all warm and tingly.

"Well, sure, of course," she mumbled. "You're rich, aren't you?"

"I suppose so. I don't think much about it."

"You don't watch much television, do you?"

"Not much. And you don't impress me as the type to watch television, either. That seems rather a tame pastime for a liberated lady plumber."

"I watched television with my mother, six years of television. I haven't always been a liberated traveling lady."

"Oh, what liberated you?"

"My mother died."

An uncomfortable silence followed Kate's statement. Max felt his throat tighten. "I'm sorry," he said softly, and touched her hand. "My mother died, too, when I was very small."

"I was twenty-four. That's when I hit the road," Kate said, allowing herself to enjoy the unexpected comfort of his touch for a moment before she pulled her hand away. "I guess I'd better go. I'm sorry about the mess. But I really do know what I'm doing, and I'll get the water temperature problem fixed as soon as I get a new shower head."

She stood up and started toward the door, stopping to retrieve the maintenance cart.

"Wait," Max said sharply. "I still don't know about Dorothea Jarrett, the lady in the wheelchair."

"Oh, yeah. Well, there was this poodle. He ran out of the hotel and caught his leash in Dorothea's wheelchair and pulled her toward your pool. She was about to take a swim with her clothes on when I stopped her chair. I couldn't take money as a reward, but she was pretty insistent. Then I found out that my car had committed suicide in your driveway. I know this must sound pretty wild to you."

"No, no it doesn't. I've had some experience with this manipulating lady. Dorothea has never been known to do anything the ordinary way if she could make it more exciting."

"Well, she convinced the manager to hire me. I'd probably never have taken the job if it hadn't been for my car. But they told me that Joe was going to be gone for two weeks and that he was your live-in maintenance man. Hey! It was fate. I fill in for Joe, get my two weeks' pay, and live in La Casa del Sol." Kate pressed the elevator button, watched the door slide silently open, and stepped inside.

"Even Kate Hepburn couldn't ask for more than that. Good night, Mr. Sorrenson. By the way, if you're going out, you'd better change your shoes."

"Why?"

The elevator door closed.

Good night? Max looked down at his watch.

Eight-thirty. Good Lord. Almost as hour earlier he'd been due to pick up Danni Manderson for dinner. Instead he'd mopped a bathroom floor, cleaned the mirrored wall, and sat at his kitchen table talking to his hotel maintenance man . . . eh, woman. He'd completely forgotten about Danni.

But he did remember that sometime during the disaster they'd just weathered, he'd considered firing Kate. Instead he'd held her hand and comforted her.

Max looked at himself in the mirrored wall of the entranceway. He was grinning like some silly yokel. Mirrors. They really were wonderful things. Walking into his study, he located his calendar and jotted down a reminder to his secretary to write to his decorator and thank her for the mirrors. He wasn't certain that he'd taken proper notice of them before.

He tried to call Danni, but she didn't answer. Feeling guilty but not knowing what else to do, Max decided to visit with Dorothea. The story of the poodle and the rescue was too intriguing for him to overlook. He went into his closet and chose a jacket. What was it Kate had said about his shoes? He looked at his feet and burst out laughing.

Max Sorrenson, who never left his apartment without coordinating his clothes, was wearing one brown loafer and one black one. He grinned, shrugged his shoulders, and exchanged both shoes for a pair of sneakers that he rarely wore. He started out the door, returned to his desk, and added a postscript to the note to his secretary.

" *Order Alpo for the poodle, who wasn't supposed to be in the hotel anyway, and . . . smaller coveralls for Kate.*"

He studied his note for a moment and scribbled again.

"Have a television set installed in the bedroom."

Almost at the elevator, he paused once more, turned, and made one final note.

"Invite Kate for dinner on Friday night."

Two

The insistent ringing of the phone awakened Kate. She sat up abruptly.

For a moment, she had forgotten where she was. She reached for the phone and put it to her ear.

"Kate, is it? This is Ricardo, the night manager. Sorry you have to start your second day on the job at five-thirty in the morning, but we have a little problem in nine-oh-four with one of our resident guests, Mrs. Jarrett. I'll meet you at the elevator."

Kate splashed cold water on her face, trying to force herself awake enough to tackle a problem. She quickly pulled on a fresh pair of Joe's coveralls and ran a comb through her hair. Heading down the sidewalk that led from the housekeeping wing to the lobby, she shivered in the gray dawn air.

"Good. That was quick," the slim, dark-skinned

man waiting by the door said in approval. "Normally Mrs. Jarrett has a companion with her, but Lucy left several days ago and isn't back yet. Mrs. Jarrett asked for you."

Kate yawned and followed Ricardo to the elevator. Mrs. Jarrett again. "What's wrong?"

"I don't know, but it sounded urgent. If you don't already know it, Mrs. Jarrett is one of our most important resident guests. She keeps things lively."

"I figured that out yesterday when she browbeat your day manager into giving me this job. Why is she in a wheelchair?" Kate asked, as much to let him know that she wasn't sleepwalking as for information.

"Arthritis, I think. She can walk with difficulty, but she uses her wheelchair most of the time. Don't let her helpless appearance fool you. She's about as innocent as a killer bee. I just hope that the problem is something we can solve."

"If it's maintenance work, I think I can handle the job," Kate replied. "I've had training in mechanics, carpentry, and plumbing. Anything else I can probably fake."

"Not necessary. We always keep three maintenance men on duty in the daytime. Anything you can't do, somebody else can. Mr. Sorrenson insists that everybody work together around here. We have a good team."

"I met Mr. Sorrenson last night. He's quite young to be so successful, isn't he? What kind of man is he?" Besides being strong, silent, sensual, and knee-knocking sexy? she added silently.

"He's pretty much a recluse. Doesn't mix much with outsiders. Just lives up there and plays with his computers, his fishing boats, and his real estate. I think he'd rather deal with spread sheets than people. He's a fair man, but he doesn't get involved. He expects us to do our jobs, and we do."

"Really?" That didn't sound much like the man she'd talked with at his kitchen table.

They reached the ninth floor, room 904. Ricardo knocked and directed his voice into a speaker panel beside the door. "It's Ricardo, ma'am, *and* Kate."

"Let Kate in. You go away."

"Yes, ma'am." Ricardo unlocked the door and gave Kate a shrug of his shoulders. It was clear that he was glad to be dismissed. "If you need help, I'll be at the desk."

Every light in the suite was burning when Kate entered. She blinked her eyes in protest and closed the door behind her. There was no sign of Dorothea.

"Mrs. Jarrett? Where are you?"

"Are you alone?"

"Yes, ma'am."

"Well, come in here. I'm in the bathroom, and I can't get this bony old body out of this damn slippery lily pond they call a hot tub."

Kate followed the voice into a bedroom-sized bath that must have been designed for some movie star out of the nineteen-forties.

Black marble tiles covered the floor and ran over the side of a lotus-shaped pool, which was filled with rose-perfumed bubbles. In the midst of the bubbles was the pink-faced cherubic woman with her arms crossed in regal disdain.

"What seems to be the problem?"

"The problem? Criminey, woman, use what sense the Lord gave you. Whoever created this swimming pool failed to take into consideration that there are those of us who need sides, normal sides. I told them I didn't want a hot tub in here anyway. Well? Don't just stand there, come and get me out."

"Come into the tub?"

"Unless you have the power to levitate."

Kate tried to keep a straight face as she considered Day Two of her grand adventure in the hotel of the rich and famous. Only a few hours earlier she'd practically drowned herself in the penthouse. Now she was about to be knee-deep in bubble bath. This was some party she'd been invited to.

Kate slipped out of her shoes, got a firm grip on her sense of humor, and stepped into the tub. She reached down to lift the slender frame of a very nude and very slippery Mrs. Dorothea Jarrett. Between the bubble bath and the downward slant of the hot tub, the chore was proving to be more difficult than she'd anticipated. She couldn't get leverage on the helpless old woman.

"How did you plan to get out?"

"I never plan. Of course, I've never used any of this bubble bath before, either. How was I to know it would make the sides slippery? If I hadn't brought my portable phone along, I'd probably be a prune by the time anybody found me."

Just as Kate thought she was making progress, her foot hit a cake of soap, and down she went, skidding into a startled Mrs. Jarrett. Water sloshed over the sides. Mrs. Jarrett was hit by a tidal wave of foam, and Kate went under like the *Titanic*.

Kate came up sputtering. As the absurdity of the scene flashed through her mind, she began to laugh. Mascara ran down Dorothea's face in wavy black lines. The older woman lifted eyelids heavy with false eyelashes and glared for a moment at

Kate before a choked-back giggle emerged like a giant hiccup.

"If this isn't a fine kettle of fish," Mrs. Jarrett said with a chuckle.

"Let me try sitting on the edge of the tub," Kate said. "I'll pull you up the side."

It worked. At least, Kate got her up the edge. Though Mrs. Jarrett was fairly light, it took lots of effort on Kate's part to get the woman into a chair.

"If you'll just hand me a towel and my robe, I'll manage. You did that rather well, considering how small you are, Kate," Mrs. Jarrett complimented her.

"I've had some experience in lifting people. My mother was an invalid for almost six years, and she had to be moved around."

"Was?"

Dorothea's question was a normal one, Kate thought, and her answer came easily for the first time. "She died two years ago."

"I'm sorry, Kate. What brought you to Florida?" Dorothea wrapped herself in the towel and began drying her face.

"Well, you remember those television commercials the temporary employment services used to run about working your way across the country? I decided if a typist could do it, so could I—three months at a time."

"Why just three months?"

"I don't want to get tied down. After twenty-four years of being in one place, I made up my mind that I would fill my life with grand adventures. By setting a time limit, I don't—won't—stay too long."

"But don't you get lonely?"

"Lonely is when you don't have friends. I have

friends everywhere. Each new job is a challenge, and I love it. Of course, my life isn't without its little problems—take my car for example. But I don't mind. You have to expect a little sour with the sweet."

"If life sends you lemons, you make lemonade. I like that philosophy. How do you like the Carnival Strip so far?"

"So far I've found it a bit wet, but once I learn my way around, I'm sure that I'm going to enjoy it."

Kate slid her hands down the legs of her coveralls, squeezing the water over the tub. She reached for a towel to blot her face as she slipped her feet back into her loafers.

"I like you, Kate Weston. I truly do. And I think I have the perfect idea."

"I'm afraid to ask." Kate gave her hair one more vigorous rub as she waited to hear Mrs. Jarrett's newest plan.

"I'm going to have the hotel manager let me borrow you for this evening. I like a person who uses lemons to make lemonade." Dorothea slapped her thigh in glee. "Yes sir-ree! I'm going to help you learn your way around. We'll have some fun. Oh, dear, you did get rather wet, didn't you?"

Kate used the wet towels to soak up the water that had spilled over the tub edge and then threw them into the hamper. "Yes, rather." Kate laughed. "But that seems to go with the job. We're both a mess. What else can I do to help you?"

"You can start by pushing me to my bed. I need to get some sleep. Don't know why I stay up so late," she said as she removed the pink shower cap and fluffed her silver hair.

Kate steadied the chair as Dorothea stood, grimaced, and swung around to lie back on her bed, still wrapped in the huge towel. "Go along with you now. I'm going straight to sleep. Just be back at eight o'clock tonight and wear a party dress. We're going to have dinner with my nephew."

"Mrs. Jarrett, I am the in-house maintenance department, and as far as I know, I'll be on duty tonight. Besides, the closest thing I own to a dinner dress is a purple satin nightgown my cousin sent me from Texas. Why on earth would you want me to have dinner with your nephew?"

"Because he needs to learn his way around too. My nephew is a stick-in-the-mud. He's very shy, never gets out. He has no fun friends. I'm dreadfully worried about him. About the only person he ever sees is me."

"Mrs. Jarrett, it would be very wrong for you to try and arrange something between me and your nephew. I'm only going to be at the hotel for two weeks, and I'm not interested in meeting a man."

"Nonsense! The hotel staff always humors me. I just pull my helpless old woman routine, and they do what I want. And I need you. Getting about without my companion isn't really safe at my age. You saw what happened yesterday."

The woman was a master, playing on Kate's guilt when she didn't appear ready to agree. Kate wondered what she'd let herself in for, then chastised herself for thinking unkind thoughts about this grandmotherly widow who had the entire hotel staff under her thumb.

"Good, it's settled. Eight o'clock tonight, Kate. You won't be sorry, I promise."

Kate wasn't certain that she'd actually agreed to go to dinner, but until she could figure out a way to outmaneuver Mrs. Jarrett, she appeared to be stuck. She locked Mrs. Jarrett's door, then punched the elevator button.

Kate realized what a sorry sight she was—her coveralls soaking wet, her hair splattered with soap bubbles. Remembering Mr. Sorrenson's request the previous night that she not be seen by the hotel guests, she hoped that it was early enough so that no one was around. If the hotel had had a service elevator, she wouldn't have had any problem, she thought as the elevator doors opened. Stepping inside, she felt an uncomfortable trickle of water run down her leg and into her shoe. Her eyes, focused on the water circling on the carpet, caught sight of a pair of familiar bare feet and legs.

The air left her lungs in a whoosh as she raised her gaze. Max Sorrenson wasn't totally nude this time, but he might as well have been. The swimsuit he was wearing was smaller than his frown.

Max Sorrenson had decided that physical exercise was the way to deal with the inexplicable frustration that kept him awake.

Dorothea had been out all evening. He couldn't seem to settle down to any serious work. By the time he'd decided to take a swim, it was early morning.

Becoming involved with an employee was something he'd never allowed himself to do. Certainly he'd never lost sight of time, missed an appointment, or put on two different shoes. In fact, Max had been careful to keep his distance from anything more than a casual relationship with a woman. It wasn't that he didn't like women. He did—very much. Or at least he enjoyed them for a time. Then, invariably, they became too posses-sive, and the time came for him to move on.

What had happened with this new employee had caught him by surprise. Until he was able to resolve the situation in his mind, he'd be unable to concentrate on anything else.

He'd spent an hour sitting at his kitchen table talking to a woman who knew more about plumbing than he did and who repaired her own auto-mobile as well. He'd be rational about this, imper-sonal. She was an employee, he wouldn't call her by name. Using her name made her real. And yet he couldn't forget how she'd stood up to him. How alive she'd been. How alive she'd made him feel.

Even as he told himself that he'd be imper-sonal, her face drifted back into focus. She'd had freckles on her cheeks, they were faint but they'd been there. She didn't need makeup to cover her flaws. There were none. Kate Weston was beauti-ful. And he knew that he wanted to see her again. The hotel was small. She'd be around some-where. Maybe she'd come back with the new shower head. Maybe he'd call her to pick up Joe's cap, which she'd left behind.

Resigned to the fact that he wouldn't accom-plish any more work, he'd finally decided that a swim might clear his mind of Kate Weston.

Resolutely pushing aside the disturbing thoughts that had plagued him for most of the night, Max pulled on a swimsuit, draped a towel around his neck, and stepped barefoot into the elevator.

The machine moved down only one floor. The door opened, and Kate Weston, the source of his consternation, stepped inside, soaking wet and dripping all over the plush carpeting.

He hadn't been prepared. His overloaded senses went into red alert, and he overreacted. What he wanted to do was kiss her. What he did was go into some marine drill sergeant's routine to cover his confusion. "That does it! Starting today," his voice vibrated across the small enclosure, "I'm having the plumbing in this entire hotel inspected."

Kate blanched. Max Sorrenson, the one person she didn't want to see, was standing there scowling. She felt her stomach do a backward somersault. Wearing nothing but a swimsuit, he looked like a candidate for a *Playgirl* centerfold. The suit was little more than a small triangle of black satin with a snip of rope to hold it on. It left nothing to the imagination. Didn't the man believe in clothes?

Kate, feeling as if she'd swallowed a sponge that was slowly expanding in her esophagus, moved into the opposite corner of the enclosure and tried not to look at Max.

"Cool down, bossman. It wasn't the plumbing this time, only a little problem with a hot tub. Bubble bath isn't a good idea in a hot tub. It makes the sides too slippery."

"Oh? Do you take many bubble baths?"

"No, never had the time. I'm a shower person. Once I camped out by a lake for two weeks. There's nothing like taking a bath in ice water every morning. Get the juices flowing."

Juices flowing? He felt as if the elevator were a blender, and his juices were being whipped into a frenzy. Picturing Kate bathing in clear lake water pushed the blender setting to full speed. He simply couldn't speak.

It was only two more floors to the lobby, Kate saw with relief, hoping her trembling legs would support her that much longer. He was apparently going out for an early morning swim—unless they were holding a Mr. America contest in the lobby.

Taking a deep breath, Max forced himself to count to ten before he finally spoke. "I trust you were able to handle the situation satisfactorily, Kate . . . Ms. Weston."

"Except for getting soaked in the process."

"I know, you're wet again," he said in a strained voice, and closed his eyes.

Kate heard the tightness in his speech. His lips were grimly pressed together, and his hands were gripping the ends of the towel fiercely.

Her gaze trailed further down his body, and she moaned at the visible expression of his discomfort straining against the fabric of his swimsuit. She was stunned. It had to be the fact that they were shut off from the world.

Sure, she thought, and the rate of her pulse was due to the hot water she'd just taken a swim in, not the man standing beside her. She had to do something, say something to diffuse the tension, or he was going to go into orbit, and she'd be right behind him.

Freckles, Max was saying to himself. He'd been right. Her face was definitely dusted with a smattering of light freckles. They were scattered across her neck and down the triangle of skin framed in the V-shaped opening of the coveralls. He groaned. His mind seemed determined to burrow beneath those coveralls no matter where he tried to cast his thoughts.

"I'm sorry about the way I look," Kate began. "I had no idea that I was going swimming, or I would have taken another uniform with me." She took a step and heard the water squish in her shoes.

"Kate." The low, controlled way he said her name seemed to be more of a caress than a rebuke. He opened his eyes and looked down at her. "You really are wet, aren't you?" He reached across and hit the stop button on the elevator panel and turned back to Kate.

Kate swallowed with difficulty. What was the man going to do, she wondered.

Max pulled the towel from around his neck and dabbed it across her forehead and cheeks. He moved it behind her ears and down her neck.

"I can't let an employee catch pneumonia," he murmured hypnotically, "not in the line of duty. What kind of an employer would I be if I didn't take care of my crew?"

Kate closed her eyes and tilted her head back so that he could wipe away the moisture. He lifted the collar of the uniform so that he could blot her shoulders and the tops of her breasts. Kate gasped.

"Are you all right, Kate?" His question was a gravelly whisper.

She opened her eyes and looked at him. All right? She didn't know. The sides of the elevator were closing in. The very air they were breathing had turned hot, and she felt as though she were going to faint.

For a moment Kate wasn't sure whether Max was going to strangle her or kiss her. Death, she decided, was only two Sylvester Stallone lips away, and she swayed toward Max. Then his arms were around her, and he began to lower his head.

"It's as warm in here as it was in Dorothea's hot tub," she blurted out as she reached up to push him away. Instead her fingers curled around his shoulders and held on.

"Yes. Dorothea," he repeated groggily.

"But once I got her out of the hot tub she was fine." Kate was rambling, not knowing what she was saying, attempting only to fill the silence. "She's some character, Dorothea. Seventy years old if she's a day, and she sleeps in the nude. Can you believe that?"

"Nude!" Kate's words pierced Max's mental fog. He shook his head as though he had been sleep-walking and slid back to clasp Kate's arms in a death grip. What was he doing? He'd almost kissed an employee in the elevator. Even now his body yearned to cover the distance he'd put between them. Stopping the elevator was a mistake. He reached behind Kate and pressed the release button. The machine began to move again.

It wasn't thoughts of Dorothea that had set off this chain reaction. It was Kate's unexpected appearance before he had been able to leash his feelings. It was the close confinement with Kate. It was because he knew that he was out of control.

The elevator doors opened and Max blinked, realizing that they could be seen. He forced himself to slow his breathing. For a long minute he looked at Kate before he released his hold on her shoulders and reached out to hold open the door.

"I'm sorry. I shouldn't have yelled at you," he said in a strained voice. "I don't often lose control like that. I certainly don't. . . . I . . . I expect that I'd better check on Dorothea. We'll talk later."

He stood stiffly, waiting for an equally stunned Kate to step outside. He jabbed at the "Close" button, muttering half under his breath. "Sexual harassment, she'll accuse you of sexual harassment. You'll be guilty as hell, and you haven't even kissed her yet."

The elevator doors had closed and the blinking

light had moved up to nine before Kate got a grip on herself. Reserved? Stuffy? The man she'd just shared the elevator with didn't seem staid to her. Uptight, maybe. Sexually repressed, perhaps. But stuffy he wasn't. He seemed more rattled than reserved. Maybe it was just her. They seemed to rub each other the wrong way.

Kate touched her shoulders where Max had held them. The coveralls were almost dry there. They had definitely heated up the elevator, she thought, and smiled. Who was she kidding? It was her own body heat that was drying her coveralls. The sight of Max Sorrenson in that swimsuit had certainly raised her temperature. She'd better find a way to avoid that man. Whenever they came together, it was volcano time.

After stopping by the laundry for a fresh supply of coveralls, Kate paused in the doorway of her room, caught by the orange streaks of a bright new day painting the sky in the east. A cool, sweet breeze held an invigorating promise, and Kate hurried to change and get ready for whatever else the day would bring.

Working at La Casa del Sol was better than taking any how-to class or watching an old movie. The only problem was that this kind of real life adventure starred a man, a man whose impact was undeniable. And men didn't play any part in the immediate future she'd planned for herself.

She wasn't the love 'em and leave 'em type. She'd loved once, but the man hadn't understood her devotion to her mother and had left.

No use dredging up old hurts, Kate decided, shaking her head. She'd loved her mother and she didn't regret that there'd only been the two of them. She didn't regret the six years she'd spent caring for her mother, either. But she didn't intend to make the mistake of falling in love. Certainly not with some reserved executive who lived in a penthouse suite.

Kate glanced around the carefully manicured hotel grounds and sighed. The quiet elegance of the old red tiled roof, the cream-colored walls, the flowers, and the white sand beach beyond had a calming effect.

Kate took a deep breath. Max was a man, and he'd reacted as a man. They'd caught each other by surprise. So what if he had wanted to kiss her? He hadn't. So what if she'd wanted him to? She was safe. After all, she was only going to be there for two weeks. The next time they met he'd probably have forgotten all about what had almost happened.

Kate was good at a lot of things, but lying wasn't one of them. Max Sorrenson might forget, but she wasn't sure that she could. It was a whole new ball game for her, and she didn't know the rules.

Wiping her face vigorously, Kate tried to erase the picture of Max from her mind, gave up, and changed into a fresh uniform. Her boss was probably the most handsome man she'd ever seen. And there was absolutely no part of him that she hadn't seen or that she didn't want to see again. *Let's face it, kid, he's probably the most exotic adventure a woman could ever have, and you're in the adventure business, aren't you?*

Kate tucked her damp hair beneath another orange cap, placed her beeper in her pocket, and made her way to the employees' dining room. She poured herself a mug of coffee and carried it out the side entrance.

Through the rose garden was a section of beach

almost hidden from the hotel by a vine-covered brick wall. The water went from transparent aquamarine to dark blue-black in the distance. Bordered by smooth white sand, clean and unmarked, the beach stretched out before her, running like a grosgrain ribbon into the gray mist. The raucous cry of the birds was the only sound as the streaks of light painted the sky. Kate sat down and leaned against the cool brick of the alcove and enjoyed the serenity of the morning.

Her mother would have liked this place and the people, Kate thought, recalling Dorothea Jarrett and her lotus-shaped hot tub. A tub like that might have soothed her mother's pain. Kate shook her head. For six years she'd done the best she knew how for her mother. Now she was doing exactly what her mother had hoped she'd do. She was getting on with her life.

Her mother had given her just one piece of advice: "Don't go out and fall in love with the first man you meet who's different, the way I did, Kate. Look around. See what the world has to offer. You're inexperienced, and you might make a mistake."

She wasn't likely to test that advice. By setting a limit on her time in one place, she didn't have to worry. She had no intention of falling in love, not for a very long time. She'd seen what could happen to a woman who fell in love with the wrong man.

Max Sorrenson was certainly the first man she'd met who was different. And he was the last man in the world she could allow herself to fall in love with—if she was interested in falling in love, which she wasn't. There might not be any such thing as a class system anymore, but he still lived in the penthouse and she lived in the maintenance wing.

Kate didn't know why she was allowing such thoughts to cross her mind. This adventure wasn't even scheduled to run her allotted three months. By the end of the week, she'd be able to buy a new water pump for the car. After the next week, she'd be mobile again. Still, the Carnival Strip was nice, and she would have a full two months left on her schedule. She might not be too quick to move on. She'd take a good look around the area first, she decided.

Kate took a sip of the coffee, which was cold now and milky brown in the cup she held absently in her hand. She heard someone headed in the direction of her hiding place and she slipped back further into the alcove.

The pounding sound of footsteps on the path told her that it was a jogger long before Max Sorrenson moved lazily past her toward the empty beach. Thank goodness he'd covered up that bathing suit with a silvery jogging suit, she thought. He stopped at the edge of a clump of palm trees and dropped his gym pants. "Oh no!" Kate muttered. He was wearing a pair of indecently fitted maroon running shorts that were even more suggestive than the bathing suit.

His jacket quickly followed his pants, and Kate was treated to the sight of his powerful chest. He draped a matching maroon towel around his neck, slipped a gray sweat band around his head and, catching the ends of the towel in his hands, started off down the beach.

"Whatever you're thinking, Kate Weston, forget it," she said out loud. She wasn't in the same league with a man like Max. She was simply working her way across the country, looking for her own place in the sun. She wasn't brilliant. She'd never been to college. The closest she'd come to culture was a dumb music appreciation course she'd started her adult education classes with—before she'd learned that pounding a hammer was more therapeutic than Mozart.

The truth was, she didn't know who she was. Maybe she didn't really want to. By not staying in one place too long she didn't have to explain anything to anybody. She could be anyone she chose to be. She could even have a grand affair, as long as she set up boundaries and time limits.

Affair? What was she thinking of? Max Sorrenson wasn't the kind of man who dallied with the hired help. He swam alone. He jogged alone. He worked alone. Kate wasn't sure whether Max would know how to dally, if the occasion presented itself. She grinned. Maybe Max needed a grand adventure. What if—what if she shared hers with him?

The powerful figure of Max Sorrenson was growing smaller in the distance. She was wrong. He wasn't a young Cesar Romero or an old Lorenzo Lamas. She'd been watching too many old movies and too much television. Max Sorrenson wasn't some cardboard character on a screen. He was a real man, who was about a million light years away from somebody like her. Too bad, she thought. Getting to know him might have been the ultimate kind of hands-on, how-to class.

Kate reluctantly turned back to the hotel. She had work to do, work that would help her gain perspective by taking her mind off the man in the penthouse suite.

Down the beach, Max was carrying on a conversation with himself as he ran, something he never did. He always felt that if a thing was important enough to do, it deserved his full attention. But today his running was automatic, and his conversation was turning into an argument.

"I need some fresh air," Max's logical self said with determination, "some exercise, that's all. It's just as Dorothea says, 'a man can't spend all his time with computers and finances without getting spooky.'

"She's a handyman, Maxwell," he argued. "She probably thinks that you're some kind of pervert, running around nude, practically undressing her in the elevator.

"Maybe," his proper self countered. "But she's honest, stood right up to you. Not many women do that. And you haven't been able to get her out of your mind. You almost kissed her. You wanted to kiss her. No, what you wanted to do was make love to her there in the hotel elevator, for heaven's sake." He ran on, his feet pounding on the damp sand.

"An employee, Maxwell, old man," Max argued, remembering how her brown eyes had sparkled with mischief. "A plumber, and she knew what she was doing. Once she has uniforms that fit, she'll be—" He stopped cold. He couldn't even argue logically with himself. Kate was an employee, and the bottom line was that he'd made a rule never to take a personal interest in an employee.

"Sure, Max, but you know your own rule—take a careful look, examine the potential, and don't let an opportunity get away from you. What you have to decide is whether Kate is an opportunity or simply a challenge."

He started off again, more slowly now that he'd stated his problem logically. If he could only come to a logical decision about how he was going to take a careful look without being burned, he'd be halfway to solving the problem.

Logic? That was a laugh. For a man who prided himself on keeping a schedule, he'd forgotten all about his plans for the evening after he'd met her. He wasn't sure that anybody would believe that he'd missed an appointment because of a feisty, brown-eyed maintenance worker.

He wasn't sure that he believed it, either.

There were two other maintenance workers on the day staff. They viewed Kate's employment with suspicion in the beginning, so she stepped back, allowing them to set the pace. The fact that she repaired the shimmy in the hotel dryer that had stymied her fellow maintenance men was a fact she kept to herself.

With no pressing duties, Kate volunteered her services to the head housekeeper. As a maid, Kate was quickly accepted. Being a maid was 'woman's work,' and she settled into the routine of stripping the beds, cleaning the rooms, and feeding soiled laundry into the huge washers.

The monotony of the chores was a blessing, for Kate couldn't keep her mind from straying back to the man in the penthouse. Never before had her thoughts been so filled by a man. Every time she stepped into the elevator, she found herself secretly hoping that he'd be inside. Every trip held a kind of intense suspense. Would he or wouldn't he remember his promise of further discussion later? And when was later?

Shortly after noon there was a lull in activity, and Kate dropped into the employee dining area to have lunch. So far, what she'd done didn't seem like work, and in spite of her dilemma, she felt a lift in her step that made her hum out loud. Every so often she forced herself to stop and examine her facial expression, fearful that she was grinning foolishly at nothing.

Kate had finished her seafood salad when the day manager, Helen Stevens, rushed into the dining room with a frantic look on her face.

"Kate, you need to get changed. I've been so busy that I forgot to tell you. You're to meet Mrs. Jarrett in the garage in half an hour. You've been released to her for the remainder of the day and evening, and you have tomorrow off."

"But I don't understand. What about my work?"

"Kate, you've already done more work last night and today than most of the crew does in a week. Besides, if Mrs. Jarrett needs you, everything else can wait."

Kate's protest that she didn't have anything suitable to wear went unanswered. Thirty minutes later, she covered her hair with a short-brimmed black hat, donned a pair of black linen tailored slacks and a plain white blouse, and left her room.

All I need is a tommy gun, and I'll look like the Godfather, Kate decided as she moved toward the garage. She hoped this excursion wouldn't take too long.

A short time later, Kate realized that unless she allowed Mrs. Jarrett to lend her the money for a dinner dress, they were likely to be there until the next week. After pushing Mrs. Jarrett through every exclusive dress shop along the Carnival Strip, Kate finally gave up and let Dorothea select a dinner gown for her. Following that ordeal, she was held hostage for two hours by a scissors-wielding blonde Viking, André the Giant, who cut and styled her hair.

Afterward she was turned over to a female version of André who created a new face for Kate. But Kate drew the line at having artificial fingernails attached to her own ragged ones. She was a maintenance worker, and those plastic things would last about five minutes. They reached a compromise with a manicure and clear polish.

Finally, Kate was allowed to view the finished product. She was thunderstruck. The dark-haired woman facing her in the mirror was stunningly alive and mysterious.

"I can't believe that's me," she whispered softly.

"It's you all right, girl. Now let's go home and get ready for that dinner party."

"I don't understand why you've gone to all this trouble just so that I can act as your companion for the evening. Probably nobody there would have noticed me."

"You'll be noticed all right. I may be a wildcatter, but I don't drill dust holes."

"If you wanted my help, fine. But all this wasn't necessary."

"Well, let's just say that I'm a meddling old woman, Kate. You remind me of myself a long time ago. Humor me, will you?"

All the way back to the hotel and up to her room, Mrs. Jarrett was quiet. She seemed lost in thought, and Kate didn't press the elderly woman. She was probably just trying to get her nephew's attention because she was lonely. She'd done Kate a good turn, and Kate couldn't be rude. What difference could it make? She'd go.

Kate stepped into the empty elevator and headed for her room. In her mind, she could see Max in his skimpy bathing suit standing there next to her.

She groaned. Her mother had never told her that there'd be days like this. And the night was yet to come.

Kate looked at herself in the mirror. The dress that Dorothea had chosen was unlike anything Kate had ever owned. The clinging blue-green garment was held at the shoulders by two mother-of-pearl shells and draped gracefully over her breasts. The resulting V-neckline would have been outrageous were it not for a silver swatch of transparent material that covered it. There was no back to the dress. The slim underskirt was slit to the thigh, revealing a scandalous expanse of bare flesh.

The hairdresser had swept her hair back behind one ear and caught it there with an alabaster shell. From the moment she'd looked in the mirror, she'd felt a strange surge of excitement. There was an aura about her that seemed to whisper of the unknown. At five minutes of eight, Kate applied fresh lipstick, a hint of fragrance, and left her room before she changed her mind and fled into the night.

Through the lobby and into the elevator she marched, determined to explain to Mrs. Jarrett her misgivings about the coming evening. She felt like a con artist involved in some great scam. This was a mistake. She'd just have to be very firm and explain that she was an employee, and the gown wasn't appropriate for a companion.

"Fiddlesticks, my dear. Lucy always dresses as if she were an invited guest. Clothes are one of the perks of her job," Dorothea told Kate moments later.

"But I'm not Lucy, and I'm certainly not an invited guest. I wear a uniform. I'm a plumber, for heaven's sake, Dorothea."

"If I'd wanted a uniformed companion, I'd have hired a police officer. You're perfect. Every man at the party will want to make love to you." Dorothea Jarrett clapped her hands in glee. "Particularly my nephew. I feel just like Henry Higgins."

"I hate to ask, but what makes you think that your nephew will be remotely interested in me? I'm certainly no Eliza Doolittle."

"Oh, but you are. You're like me, Kate. You're a real flesh-and-blood woman, not some cardboard character with ice water in her veins."

"Ice water?" Max Sorrenson flashed immediately into Kate's mind. Too bad the bossman couldn't step onto the elevator and see her as she looked tonight. *Get real, Kate,* she told herself. Max Sorrenson probably wouldn't have recognized her anyway.

"Let's hit the road, Kate, my girl. We're going to cause a bigger fire than Mrs. O'Leary's cow. If I don't miss my guess, there'll be a hot time in the old town tonight."

Eliza Doolittle, Mrs. O'Leary's cow, and a reclusive nephew about to be shook up. Five minutes with Dorothea Jarrett, and Kate's head was whirling. There was a nagging thought that she was missing something important in what Dorothea had just said.

Kate pushed the wheelchair into the elevator and took a good look at her companion's outfit, privately agreeing that the purple gown with the feather boa might cause a riot.

Mrs. Jarrett caught her expression and winked. "I know. It looks like something Mae West might have worn, doesn't it? Why do they think that old ladies and hookers wear only purple? Personally, I'd rather have red sequins or pink satin. I saw a wonderful black satin bodysuit with an overblouse. They're ordering it for me in cerise."

The elevator started up. "Sorry, Mrs. Jarrett, I forgot to hit the button. Where are we going?"

"Call me Dorothea, and we're there."

The door was opening.

"But this is the penthouse. Max Sorrenson, the hotel owner, lives here."

"He certainly does."

"But . . . your nephew might not mind, but what will Mr. Sorrenson think about you bringing me along?"

"But, Kate, I thought you knew," Dorothea said with a wicked glint in her eyes. "Max Sorrenson *is* my nephew."

Three

Any hopes Kate might have had of hovering innocently in the background were dashed when they left the elevator and Max's dark eyes locked onto her like laser beams. The force of his gaze was a frightening assault on her senses, and she held onto Mrs. Jarrett's wheelchair, using it as a shield before her.

"Hello, my love," Max Sorrenson's words were for Mrs. Jarrett, but his attention was on Kate until he was directly before them.

After a pregnant moment of silence he dropped his glance affectionately to his aunt, freeing Kate from the numbing inertia that had engulfed her.

He was leaning over, holding his aunt's hands tenderly as she chattered an answer to a question that Kate hadn't heard. Kate had known that accompanying Mrs. Jarrett would be a bad idea. She just hadn't known how bad.

Why wasn't he saying something? Was it possible that he didn't recognize her? He'd only seen her in coveralls, looking like something the cat dragged in. Tonight her appearance was very different. Tonight she was different. Dorothea had seen to that. But she was still a hotel employee masquerading as a guest.

Kate wanted desperately to step back into the waiting elevator and head down to a level where her breath would be even once more. The feeling was so compelling that she made an involuntary backward motion, the faint suggestion of movement invoking a quick retort from Mrs. Jarrett.

"Forward, Kate. We're attacking, not retreating."

"Attacking? What is this, dear aunt, some *grand adventure* you're planning? If so, I insist on being allowed to take part."

Grand adventure? He knew. He remembered what she'd said about her life's goal. There was no doubt about it, he recognized her. Any minute now he'd expose her. She'd be embarrassed. Dorothea would be embarrassed. She had to figure out some way to make a quiet exit—fast.

"Of course, nephew. We wouldn't think of leaving you behind. You might say that you're smack dab in the middle of our adventure."

Kate groaned. It wasn't bad enough that Dorothea agreed. She'd made him the focus of the situation. Dorothea couldn't have made it any plainer that she was dangling Kate before him.

Max Sorrenson drew back and stopped, trying to keep a stern expression on his face. It wouldn't do to let his aunt know that he was glad to see Kate. Dorothea had hinted recently that she was going to find a woman for him. He ought to be angry at her meddling. He could tell her that he and Kate were already acquainted, but why spoil what promised to be an exciting evening?

All day he'd wandered around the hotel, trying unsuccessfully to run into Kate Weston accidentally. And here she was, in his apartment, looking as if she'd like to disappear in a cloud of smoke.

Of course he'd recognized Kate immediately. But her new look had thrown him. Skillfully applied makeup had turned eyes that had sparkled with fire into dark orbs of mystery. The same dark hair that had dried into a feathered crown was now swept exotically back from her face on one side and caught by a shell comb. She'd been beautiful before. But tonight she seemed to shimmer with magic.

It occurred to him briefly that the rescue, the job, and their meeting might all have been part of a plan by his diabolical aunt. If something bizarre happened, he could always count on Dorothea being at the center of the occurrence. The fact that his aunt had managed to avoid him for the past two days added fuel to the fire. For once he didn't care. He was more than willing to play along.

Still, he was surprised at Kate's complicity. Her appearance as a guest at his dinner party seemed out of character. He would have bet that the woman he'd seen on her hands and knees in his bathroom was incapable of deception. He would also wager that she was an innocent victim of Dorothea's maneuvering.

Kate moistened her lips uneasily with her tongue. Disaster was at hand. Max was openly appraising her. Her pulse fluttered unevenly as she forced herself to meet his gaze.

She hadn't known that Max was Dorothea's nephew, but, looking back, the connection should have been obvious. If she hadn't been so preoccupied, she'd have put it all together. But she knew now and she had to break the tension. Kate tilted her head and gave him her most challenging smile. Let him open, as Dorothea would say, "the can of worms."

Max returned her smile. He'd expected the evening to be the usual boring dinner party. Suddenly it had become intriguing. He'd play along with the charade until he could find out what Dorothea was up to. He didn't want to spoil her fun, he told himself, knowing that his excuse was a lie.

"And do I know your partner in crime, Aunt Dorothea?"

"Perhaps, perhaps not," Mrs. Jarrett said airily, an unmistakable sparkle shining in her soft blue eyes.

"I'm sure I would remember if we'd met before," Max said, "I have a good memory for faces."

Faces? Kate didn't answer. It wasn't a face that flashed through her memory. It was a nude body that made her muscles contract and her chest constrict.

Tonight Max was fully clothed. He was wearing a black dinner jacket that emphasized his broad shoulders, tapered waist, and the dark hair curling against the neck of his starched white pleated shirt. He'd gone from *Playgirl* centerfold to *Esquire* model in a matter of hours. Yuppie of the decade. Everything about him was perfectly coordinated, even down to—she glanced at his feet—his polished black dress shoes.

He caught her eye and nodded. He knew exactly what she'd been thinking. It was time that she swallowed the lump in her throat and let him know that she could play his game too. She wouldn't have been here if she'd known. But here she was, and there was no way she was going to back down to Max Sorrenson.

Their forward progress had stopped in the foyer, just outside the living room filled with people who were staring at them curiously. She'd heard enough to know how private Max was. He wouldn't welcome her confession before his guests even if she'd been inclined to make it. Harassment went two ways, she decided. It was her turn to have a little fun.

"I don't know," Kate murmured disinterestedly, "I meet so many people in my line of work. It does seem to me that we've met. I just can't recall where."

"Maybe I look like someone you know, some television star," Max commented in amusement. "I've been told that I remind people of some young hunk."

"Max!" Dorothea scolded. "Where are your manners? Is this some kind of game you're playing?"

"I thought you told me your nephew was a stuffy, uptight, lonely man. I think he's quite . . . interesting," Kate said, easily reading the hidden meaning of their conversation.

"Oh? And what else have you concluded about me?"

"That you're a man who knows how to dress. By the way, I like your shoes. They do match your outfit very well." Dorothea twisted her head slightly and glanced back at Kate.

This time Max couldn't conceal his delight. Fine. They were on the same wavelength. The only person not aware of the current flashing between them was Dorothea, and from the curious look on her face, he thought she might be a little suspicious. Dorothea had gone quiet, too quiet and too content to be left out of their conversation.

"You have a lovely apartment, Max . . . I mean Mr. Sorrenson." Kate glanced around.

"It looked quite different last night, when it was ankle-deep in water," he said coolly. "But I'm pleased you like it Ms. . . ? What did you say your name was?"

"Kathryn," Dorothea suddenly joined in. "Kathryn Weston. Kathryn is new in the area. Do move aside Max, I'd like to introduce Kathryn to your guests."

"Odd," Max persisted as he stepped to the side of his aunt's wheelchair. "I don't recall hearing you mention Ms. Weston before. Do you like the ocean, Kathryn? You look like a water person to me."

"Yes, I do like the ocean," Kate said. "But somehow you look more like a valley person to me. Do you by any chance grow grapes?"

"No, do you think I should?"

There was no sense of anger in his teasing. Rather, a euphoric sense of pleasure seemed to have enfolded them, and Kate felt the last of her uneasiness being replaced with excitement. She could stand her ground with Max. It was the others she wasn't sure about.

But Dorothea was right. This was an adventure, one she'd never have again. Tonight she'd let the current carry her along. The only problem was that the current crackled, and she was afraid that an innocent bystander might move between them and be electrocuted by mistake. Controlling that kind of electricity was something they never covered in her how-to class.

"Max, my dear nephew," Dorothea said smugly, "we do appreciate your attention, but this entranceway is becoming a bore. Are you planning to let us in, or will we be served on trays in the elevator?"

"Do forgive me, my love." He took a step forward. "Please come in. I'd like to show Kathryn my apartment. I have a particularly nice bathroom and walk-in closet." He made a motion to relieve Kate of the wheelchair, brushing her hand with his fingertips.

Kate jerked her hand away, causing the chair to shimmy for a moment.

"Oh?" She recovered quickly and asked, "Do you have mirrors? I'm partial to mirrors in my dressing area." Max swallowed hard. *One for me*, she thought.

Gripping the handles of Mrs. Jarrett's chair, Kate had no intention of giving up the barrier between herself and the man beside her. She'd already found out what happened when they were alone together. As long as she had something to hold on to, she wouldn't float across the floor.

Kate followed Max through the foyer, past the door to his bedroom, and into the main living area. An assortment of elegantly dressed people were standing in small groups, chatting noisily.

"Dorothea!" A white-haired, bearlike man roared from across the room. "Come and tell me what exciting things you're cooking up tonight."

Kate followed Mrs. Jarrett's nod of agreement and pushed the chair toward the man, relieved to note that someone else had caught Max's attention. Now her over-sensitive nerve endings had time to calm down. She'd obviously been optimistic in believing that he'd ignore her the next time they met.

Kate hadn't been in this part of Max's apartment before. The suite was decorated in cream and gray. The colors might have been too neutral were it not for the vivid splashes of blues and greens in the ocean paintings and nautical wall hangings. The room was L-shaped, with glass walls on one side that opened onto a wraparound balcony overlooking the Gulf and the bright lights of the Carnival Strip, which sparkled like some garish piece of costume jewelry in the night.

"Kathryn," Dorothea trilled, "come and meet this old sea pirate, Matthew Blue, my closest friend. Second-best fisherman I ever knew, till he swapped his fishing nets for paintbrushes and canvas."

"How do you do, Mr. Blue. Paintbrushes? Are you an artist?"

"Well," he said with a chuckle. "I dabble a little."

"Nonsense," Dorothea stated emphatically, "Matthew's like me—never did a little bit of anything in his life. He's responsible for all these pictures on Max's walls."

Kate would have liked to examine the paintings more closely. She wanted desperately to slip into the background, but even with her back turned, she was conscious of being watched. She knew that Max was still staring at her from across the room, and she trembled.

"Where on the seven seas did you find this delicious pearl?" Matthew was asking Dorothea.

"Oh, Matthew, this is Kate, eh, Kathryn, and you wouldn't expect me to give away my best fishing holes, now, would you?" Dorothea laughed.

"Of course not. Watching you keep secrets is one of the bright spots in my life since they won't let me go to sea anymore. So tell me, Kathryn, what do you like to do for fun?"

"Oh, please, I'd rather know about you," Kate said. "You were a sailor?"

"Indeed I was, and a shrimper, before this old body ran out on me. Dottie, Walt, and I were the three best fishermen on the Gulf Coast. Now Walt's gone, Dottie's landlocked, and all I do is make pictures of what I see in my soul."

"Pictures of the soul. What a lovely way to express it," Kate said. "I've never been around the sea before, but I already love it. I'd like to have been a pirate, I think, to sail the sea searching for treasure."

"The feel of the spray on your face, and the north star at your back? Very poetic, Ms. Weston," Max Sorrenson commented, holding out one of the two glasses he was carrying. "Here you are Auntie, a tonic water with a twist of lemon for you. I took the liberty of bringing the same for you, Kathryn. Somehow you look like a person who prefers water to alcohol. And Kathryn sounds much too formal. May I call you Kate?"

"Of course, and thank you." Kate answered with artificial politeness in her voice. "And I do find the slice of lemon just the right touch."

"Oh, you like things a bit tart, do you?"

"Now, Max," Dorothea interrupted, unable to disguise her puzzlement. "I'm surprised at your bad manners. I've promised Kathryn that this is just the right place to add a little sweetness to her life."

"Oh? Well, my dear aunt, let us find out. Are you Kate, as in the strong-minded Kate Hepburn? Or are you the fiery, exciting shrew Mr. Shakespeare wrote about."

"Neither," Kate answered, a bit unevenly, "I'm just plain Kate, as in Weston."

Max tried to tell himself that it was the change in appearance that made Kate so exciting. But he'd found the woman in coveralls the night before just as intriguing. He searched her face over the top of his glass as he took a sip, trying to find an answer to this compelling fascination he was experiencing.

Logically, he recognized that she wasn't the type of woman he normally liked. She was too undisciplined, moving from one place to another with no plan for her life. She was much too cheeky, calling him "bossman" and insisting that he help her repair the plumbing. He'd never met anyone quite so dauntless. Now she'd teamed up with Dorothea for goodness knew what. Kate Weston was definitely dangerous.

He continued to study her until he realized that the others were looking at him expectantly. What had just been said? Something about Kate being plain? Yes, that was it.

"Plain? I think not," Max grinned, a teasing promise in his smile. "Definitely not plain. And I think I'm going to have fun discovering who the real Kate is."

In spite of herself, Kate felt her heart pound and her face turn flame red. Hurriedly, she took a sip of her drink and knew as soon as she swallowed, that it had gone down wrong.

Matthew sprang to her side with a napkin as she began to cough. By the time the choking attack had passed, the conversation seemed forgotten.

"Have you done any sailing, Kate?" Matthew asked.

Kate was grateful for his question. "Absolutely none at all."

"So you think you'd like sailing and the sea?" Max perched lazily on the sofa arm and openly examined Kate. "I ought to show you my boat. As a matter of fact, that's a good idea. I'll take you sailing tomorrow. I have a committee meeting in Panama City. We'll sail down and do some sight-seeing along the way."

For once Dorothea seemed content to sit as quiet as a stump. From the puzzled expression she wore, Kate knew that she was picking up on the under-currents in Max's innocent-sounding statements.

"Oh, no. I'm sorry. I couldn't," Kate blurted out much too quickly, then searched for an accept-able reason to decline. Exchanging verbal repar-tee was one thing, but a date with the boss? No.

Kate could tell from Max's expression that he wasn't accustomed to being turned down, and from the stern narrowing of his lips, she knew that he wasn't about to drop his invitation. "I have to work," she added quickly.

"Work? That's intriguing. Precisely what kind of work do you do, Kathryn? I'm very interested."

"She's a—a writer," Dorothea interjected smugly.

"Oh?" Max lifted an eyebrow, trying to smother a smile as he caught Kate's look of dismay. "And what do you write?"

"I'd—I'd rather not discuss my work now," Kate stammered, secretly shooting a look of fury at Mrs. Jarrett, who seemed to be thoroughly enjoy-ing her discomfort. "My work is rather . . . differ-ent from what all these people might expect," she finished sternly.

"A writer, how exciting," one of the other guests commented.

"What are you, a critic?" another asked. "Have you brought one of those people who rates the hotel into our midst, Dorothea?"

"Certainly not! Really, Mrs. Jarrett," Kate shot Dorothea a look intended to straighten her hair and curl her toes. "Tell him the truth."

"My aunt tell the plain truth?" Max shook his head. "Never happen. Never in her lifetime has she told a simple fact if she could embroider it with exaggeration."

"Nonsense, Max. That's your problem. You're a 'just the facts, ma'am' person."

"What I am," Kate interjected sharply, "is—"

"Oh, don't tell me," Max said smoothly, "let me guess. Somehow, you don't look like a travel writer who's reviewing the hotel incognito. But people do disguise themselves in the most creative ways to get what they want," Max said in a voice that dared her to correct him, a voice that reached out and touched her like a physical caress.

"Sometimes people end up in situations they didn't plan on," Kate said steadily, hoping that Max would let the matter drop.

"Don't hold back, Kate. If you're truly interested in my place, I'll take you on a guided tour myself, anything you want to see. Of course the plumbing is undergoing some renovation at the moment."

"Plumbing? Dull, nephew. You have no imagination. Kate's not spying on the hotel. She's a writer on the staff of . . . *Maverick* magazine for men," Dorothea added triumphantly, sipping her drink with a rakish gleam in her eyes.

"*Maverick?*"

Max's startled look and the ensuing silence were new threats ready to fall. Kate couldn't allow this to go any further. Teasing Max was a great deal of fun, but Dorothea's plan was getting out of hand.

"Mr. Sorrenson," Kate began. "I'd like to talk to you privately."

"Of course you would, Kate, and Max wants to talk to you too," Dorothea agreed with a broad wink, "and you will, right after dinner. Look, the waiter is trying to catch your eye, Max. I'm starved. How about it, everybody? Let's eat!"

"Why not?" Max nodded and moved through the sliding glass doors to the largest table. "Will you sit at my table, Dorothea? Or shall I send you to sit in the corner like the bad girl you are?"

"With you, of course," Mrs. Jarrett answered, wearing the same angelic smile Kate had witnessed when she'd seen the woman sitting arms crossed and nose high in a tub full of pink bubble bath the night before. "I promise I'll be good. I wouldn't miss this lovely dinner for the world."

Heavy cut glass containers held fat candles that cast a myriad of silver sparkles across the lavender twilight. Creamy white gardenias floated in bowls of shimmering water. The smell of the ocean wafting in the breeze mingled with the sweet scent of the gardenias and seemed to curl romantically about the candle flame, causing it to wax and wane in the darkness.

Max Sorrenson took Kate's elbow and brought her to the table. His hand set off an involuntary tingle, and she started, unconsciously rubbing away the sensation.

"Kate, my girl," Matthew Blue pulled up the chair next to her. "I insist on sitting beside you. Bring on the food, Max. Dorothea looks as if she's about to devour the centerpiece."

"Nothing my aunt does surprises me." Max planted an innocent kiss on her forehead.

Kate could see that the tenderness of the kiss didn't match the warning in his eyes as he settled down in the seat across from Kate.

"Now, Max," Dorothea admonished. "Don't get a burr under your saddle. You always get cross when you aren't running the show. You'll scare

Kate to death. And Matthew, you're much too old for that child. Stop flirting with her, or you'll make me very jealous."

"Kate doesn't impress me as the type that scares easily, Aunt Dorothea," Max said smoothly. Dorothea was right. He did tend to become gruff when he was thwarted. It was a kind of defense mechanism that he'd learned as a child. "I can't wait to read your column, or is it adventure articles you do?"

"I don't write a column," Kate said. "I'm more into how-to projects."

"You mean like do-it-yourself plumbing?"

"Don't be silly, Max. Does Kate look like a plumber?"

"Oh, I think she could be. I don't know about Kathryn, but Kate—now that's another story. Kate intrigues me greatly."

"Wonderful!" Dorothea's shout of approval met with a raised eyebrow from her nephew. "I mean the food is wonderful."

The salad was followed by the entrée of tender medallions of veal, and finally the dessert, raspberry sherbert, was served.

"Personally," Dorothea confided, glancing smugly toward Kate, "I prefer lemon sherbert, provided it's sweet enough. But raspberry is nice too."

"So, Kathryn," Max finally said, after listening to the discussion of the merits of lemon over raspberry sherbert, "what kind of assignment are you on? I mean currently, of course."

"Oh, Max. You always were too inquisitive, even as a small boy. Then I'd just swat you on the bottom, and you'd stomp back up to your room and slam the door. Never could get him to get out and get dirty like a normal boy."

"How long will it take, this secret assignment of yours?" Max persisted.

Dorothea rolled her eyes but kept silent.

Max didn't know why he persisted in his attempt to force Kate to admit that they'd met. Maybe it was because Kathryn, this new person she'd become, so unsettled him.

Max liked Kate, the woman who'd yelled at him, forced him to hold the wrench while she deftly took care of a problem that would have made most women start to cry. The woman across the table from him was Kathryn, and Kathryn was an enigma.

Kate was easy, fun, appealing. Kathryn, on the other hand, was mysterious, exciting, a woman he couldn't seem to catalog. One thing he was certain of was that he was having more fun than he'd had in a very long time. How long, he wondered, would his aunt allow this little game to continue?

Kate pretended to enjoy her meal. She knew that Max was staring at her. He knew she was Kate the handyman, not a writer for some magazine. But the person at this table wasn't Kate. The person lifting her wineglass was Kathryn, and Kathryn wasn't going to give an inch. She'd stay on this carousel as long as Max wanted to continue the ride.

"How long will my assignment take? I haven't any idea," Kate answered. "I'd planned on two weeks with pay. But since my cover has been blown, that could end. Some people think that my employer is something of a snob, accustomed to throwing his weight around. If that turns out to be true, I may be expendable."

"A snob? I disagree," Max said briskly. "Sometimes people in authority get pigeonholed and don't know how to change their images. Maybe you ought to stand up to the man. Maybe he likes a woman with spirit."

Their eyes met across the table. Kate could see a grudging respect in his gaze. She smiled. Their first encounter had been declared a draw.

"Perhaps I will," Kate said, lifting her glass in an unspoken salute.

Max smiled and lifted his glass, returning the tribute.

As coffee was being poured, Matthew leaned back, lit a long thin cigar, and put a serious expression on his face. "With all your money tied up, Max, how are you fellows at the Hotel Association going to handle the outsiders? Slowly but surely they're moving in. Frankly, I don't want them here, any of them."

Max shook his head and frowned. "Now, Matt, all of us were outsiders once. Thank goodness there were those willing to accept us, or we wouldn't be here."

"True," Dorothea agreed. Some kinds of change ought to be welcomed. There are just some of us too stubborn to admit it."

"Seriously, Matt," Max went on, "over-fishing the Gulf is a problem. We may be able to head off any fisherman not yet here, but those already licensed are legal. As for the Hotel Association, as long as current hotel owners give the committee first refusal on the sale of any property, we can buy the hotels, then resell them to acceptable owners. That's the only way we can keep organized crime and gambling out of our family resort area."

"Well, maybe. The shrimp are practically all gone. And if the king mackerel count falls off any more,

I don't know. A man's got to fill his net one way or the other."

"Exactly my thought," Dorothea exclaimed, and yawned noisily. "Every man ought to fill his net. My goodness, Kate, I'm just about to fall asleep. I think we'd better go."

"The late hours and the schedule you keep, no doubt," Max observed shrewdly. "But that's no reason for Kate to go. There's still time for dancing, maybe a midnight breakfast and a stroll to watch the sun rise."

"Not tonight, Max. Kate has other . . . obligations. Maybe tomorrow. Good night, Matthew. Lovely party, Max. Don't let us break up the evening."

Kate quickly rose and took Dorothea's chair. Feeling Max's gaze on her all the way to the elevator, she gave a Joan Crawford shift to her shoulder and fought the urge to look back.

"Where can I reach you in the morning, Kathryn, to let you know what time we're leaving?"

"Just call me," Dorothea answered quickly. "I'll relay any message."

"Fine, I'll call you first thing in the morning, Dorothea," Max said.

When the elevator doors closed behind them, Kate let out a deep sigh of relief. The evening had been unreal. She still didn't know why Max hadn't told Dorothea that he knew who she really was. But now the evening was over, and she wasn't sure where she stood. If she was fired, she was fired. Nothing was going to change that.

What she wouldn't do was let him drive her away. What she couldn't do was admit that he was more than just an exciting, desirable man. She didn't have to be Deborah Kerr or Bette Davis to feel herself responding. She leaned on the wheelchair, feeling it move under the force of her pressure.

"What's the matter, girl, don't have your 'sea legs' under you yet? The phone is ringing. Wonder who that could be?"

Kate opened Dorothea's door and stood, waiting to bolt as soon as Dorothea was safely inside.

"Hold on a minute, Kate, while I answer this. Hello? Probably. I heard you, Max. Yes, I know that Kate didn't give you an answer. Yes, she's here. I'll tell her. Good night, Max." Dorothea turned back to Kate, rubbing her hands in undisguised glee.

"Good night, Dorothea," Kate began.

"That was Max. Wanted to be sure that you weren't leaving? He seemed to think that you might panic and check out. I told him that you'd still be here tomorrow. I suppose Joe's room is technically 'here.' "

"Dorothea, after the wild things you told him tonight, I don't know why you'd worry about technicalities. I think that there is something you'd better know before this gets any more insane. Your nephew knows who I am."

"Of course he does. I told him your name."

"No, he knows that I work for him in the maintenance department. I repaired a leak in his bathroom last night."

"So that's what all that sizzle was about tonight. I get the distinct feeling that there was more than plumbing involved."

"There wasn't! Of course, I've never worked around a naked man before. But I got the job done."

"Naked man? Wonderful! I don't even want to

know what that means. It worked. Even I couldn't have set up a more exciting scenario. And he's already called here to make sure you're going with him tomorrow." Dorothea removed the cape of her gown and trailed the feathers under her chin and across her bosom.

"He's probably going to put me before the firing squad at dawn, Dorothea. That's why he wants to be sure that I'm where he can find me."

"Oh, I don't think so. But that does explain why he said that Errol Flynn wasn't the only pirate to sail the southern seas. Oh, Kate," Dorothea said, "it's intrigue that gives life it's flavor. Don't you want to have a little excitement in your life?"

"Excitement, yes. That's why I'm working my way across the country. But I didn't take a how-to class in playing games."

"Oh, but you don't need lessons, Kate. You have a natural talent. I'm a good judge of people, and I understand you and Max very well. An adventure is a lot more fun if you have someone to share it with. Go with Max tomorrow."

Maybe Dorothea was right. She was only going to be there for two weeks. Why not enjoy being a part-time mystery woman? Still, she didn't want to make it too easy on the septagenarian. Let her enjoy the challenge. Maybe Dorothea needed a little sugar in her lemonade too.

"All right, I'll think about it. But the bottom line is that I'm a maintenance worker, and I'm afraid that sooner or later Max is going to be furious with you about this."

"Nonsense. Max may not have my sense of humor, but he's got my blood in him."

"But—" Kate began once more.

"No, no more buts. Not tonight. Go to bed, Kate."

Mrs. Jarrett softened the expression on her face and squeezed Kate's hand. "Please, humor me. And soon I'll tell you about another woman who was given the chance to share a grand adventure."

The shower water was hot and it felt wonderful. Afterward, Kate fell wearily across her bed, on the edge of falling asleep.

She wasn't sure why she let herself turn into Kathryn. She must have been under some sort of magical spell. The morning light would erase that soon enough. She was a maintenance worker with leaky faucets and faulty TVs to repair, not some foxy lady on an assignment. Still, for one magic moment Kate had become the mysterious Kathryn, pursued by an executive who lived in a penthouse suite.

Four

Kate awoke suddenly, jarred by the urgent pounding on her door. She groaned and willed the person to leave. He didn't.

The person at the door had to be Max, she
realized. Any hope she had that he had forgotten
about the previous night and would go to his
committee meeting in Panama City without her
evaporated.

"Go away!" she yelled desperately. "I'm busy!"

"Doing what?"

"Sleeping." It was Max, and she wasn't ready to
face him.

"Not any more," he said.

"No, your pounding woke me up."

There was a moment of silence. "I can think of
better ways to do it, if you'll open this door."

His voice was hoarse and a bit unsteady. Kate
clutched the sheet tightly as if it might restrain
her from flinging open the door and wrapping
herself in his arms.

On the other side of that door, Max realized that things weren't working out the way he'd planned—if he'd had a plan, which he hadn't. He'd ordered a picnic lunch, canceled it, and ordered it again. This trip was business. Taking her along on his boat would be a distraction when he needed to concentrate on the upcoming meeting.

But leaving her behind would be an even bigger distraction. What he wanted to do was cancel the meeting and take Kate straight to his apartment—and make love to her.

Such intense desire for a woman was new to him, and he'd spent half the night trying to understand it. Finally, at dawn, he'd decided to go without her. Yet there he was, outside Kate's door. When she'd yelled that she was sleeping, all thoughts of leaving without her vanished.

"Kate, will you let me in?"

"No! I'm . . . I'm not dressed."

Ahhh! She was lying in bed naked not three feet away. Max groaned again.

Let him in? Kate's mind seized on the picture of Max waking her up, seized on it and expanded it in less than a second. Weakly she sighed, recognizing the beginning of an ache in her head and a tingle between her thighs that seemed to be an automatic response to his presence.

For Pete's sake. She was no virgin, though her experience had been limited and long ago. But Max Sorrenson was an assault on her senses that she couldn't stave off. Sylvester Stallone lips, a Chuck Norris body, and the sophistication of Cary Grant. He was a man to die for—but not to open the door for.

"I'm sure you're more alarming than a clock, Max, but no thanks. If you don't intend to fire me after last night's little escapade, I think I'd better go to work. Plumbing is a lot safer than being alone with you."

"Work? Not today. I've arranged for the boss to give you a day off. It seems a new employee has converted him to the theory that all work and no play makes Max a dull boy."

Then she wasn't out of a job. She leaned back on her pillow and tried to suppress the unexpected happy feeling that came over her. She allowed herself to consider the possibility of going with Max, of the two of them sailing down the coast like ordinary people on a Sunday cruise.

But, no. She doubted that they'd get out of the harbor. Kate swung her feet to the floor and sat up. She wanted to go with Max Sorrenson. There was a sense of power about him that was intoxicating. But he was the man in the penthouse, and she knew that she belonged there about as much as beer in the boardroom.

"Max, it wouldn't be smart for me to go with you."

"At least let's talk about it."

He wasn't going to give up. Sooner or later somebody else in the hotel was going to see or hear him pounding on her door. "All right," she agreed, "I'll come to your office and discuss the situation."

Max had heard her voice change from dreamy to irritated to resigned. Irritation was an emotion that could be teased into excitement. But resignation was more difficult to deal with. *There you go again Sorrenson*, he told himself, *you're being stuffy*. He wanted to hear the dreamy voice again, and he didn't know how to coax it back.

Maybe he could challenge her. Maybe she wouldn't be able to resist replying to the kind of lighthearted banter they'd exchanged the previous night.

"Good. I'm always willing to hear any employee's grievance. Never let it be said that Max Sorrenson isn't open to compromise," he ad-libbed. *That ought to do it.* "I'll meet you in my office in ten minutes."

His office? Too late she remembered that Max's office was in his penthouse suite. She'd be the one who was compromised. "No. I think that would be a mistake. I'll met you in the manager's office, or," she announced bravely, "or not at all."

"That isn't a good idea, Kate. There are too many people there. I really think we ought to keep this discussion private."

He was right. How would it look to have an audience when the pompous eccentric and his plumber discussed their impossible relationship? Kate couldn't hold back a smile. She was beginning to realize that Max and his aunt were alike, even if they didn't recognize their similarities. They were both a bit daft.

First Dorothea had forced her into a situation where she didn't belong, now Max was doing the same. It didn't make sense for him to be interested in her. He should be able to see that there was no future for them. She was only there temporarily.

Kate wrapped the sheet around her, came to the door, and leaned her head against it. "Please, Max. Last night was a mistake. I didn't know that you were Mrs. Jarrett's nephew when I agreed to go with her. I was out of line. Just go away and leave me here to do my work. Don't make this into something that it isn't."

An irrational flash of anger roared through Max.

He was known as the man who was always in control. Yet this time he couldn't stop his words. "All right. Let me put it another way, Ms. Weston. You will get dressed and sail down the coast with me, or there will be two unemployed people in this hotel by noon. You and the day manager who hired you."

Kate opened the door. "You wouldn't dare! It isn't Helen Stevens's fault. Your aunt browbeat her into giving me this job. What kind of man are you?"

She was wrapped in a thin sheet. He could see the shape of her small breasts with their dark nipples jutting proudly beneath the fabric. Her hair was softly tousled, and her eyes sparkled defiantly.

Max swallowed hard. He'd done it now. He'd made himself into Simon Legree when all he'd wanted to be was Lorenzo Lamas. She should never have opened the door. "An impatient one," he said, biting off the words with clenched teeth. "And you're right. I'm not going to fire Helen. Because you're coming, if I have to kidnap you. Fifteen minutes. In front of the hotel. And, Kate, do put on something that will cover that body, or we may never get off the boat."

Kate knew she had no choice. She looked down at her body and back at the man. She'd never thought much about how she looked. Back in Kentucky she was accepted for who she was. Since leaving home she'd had to fight so hard to prove that she was able to do a man's job that she'd grown used to rough talk and sexual innuendo. She'd always become just one of the boys. But Max didn't see her that way. And when he looked at her, her body reacted in very feminine ways.

Even now her sensitive nipples were responding to the rough touch of the fabric rubbing against them as she breathed. "I'll be there," she said in a whisper.

"I'm glad." The dreamy quality was back in her voice, and Max felt a warm sense of possessiveness swell inside him. Another minute and that wouldn't have been the only thing that swelled.

Kate splashed her face with water, ran a comb through her hair, and turned to the closet to survey her wardrobe. Cover her body? Fine. She tugged on the pair of faded jeans she'd been wearing the last time she worked on the car. Battery acid had eaten holes in the legs, and there was a three-cornered tear in the knee. She pulled a grease-smeared T-shirt emblazoned with the Atlanta Braves logo over her head and stuck her feet into sneakers with holes. As a last glowing touch, she crammed the orange cap on her head. She looked like a slob. That ought to keep him from forcing her to go, she decided.

Kate rounded the corner of the building and caught her breath. The grim expression on Max's face and the sight of his clenched fists made her chest tighten and her stomach flutter. Unsuccessfully, she fought back an attack of panic, then ducked into the souvenir shop, rubbing the goose bumps that had suddenly raised like ant hills down her arms.

"May I help you?" The sales clerk hovered near the entrance, obviously suspicious of the oddly dressed woman hiding behind a rack of sunglasses.

"Ah, yes," Kate stammered, desperately wishing that she had never turned her automobile into the driveway of La Casa del Sol. She saw Max plowing through the lobby in her direction. He'd seen her.

"I'd like these," she said as she searched the rack wildly, selecting a pair of over-large bright yellow plastic sunglasses.

"Kate!"

She jammed the glasses on her nose and turned to face him.

"What are you doing, and why are you dressed like a refugee from a thrift store? Never mind." He took her hand and drew her unyieldingly toward the front door.

"Ma'am? Excuse me, ma'am?" The clerk was scurrying behind them like a bird uncertain of her perch.

"Yes? What in blazes do you want?" Max roared.

"The glasses, sir. There is a ten-dollar charge for the glasses the lady bought."

"Ten dollars? If those awful things cost ten dollars, I can understand why you have so many of them. Tell Helen Stevens to write a charge off and put those tacky things on sale immediately."

"Yes, sir." The puzzled clerk was unsure of what was happening, but she was beginning to understand that the man directing her was someone in charge. "What shall we price them at, sir?"

"Give them away if you have to. Just get rid of them." He was doing it again. He was acting like a jerk, he realized.

"Max!" Kate protested. "She's only doing her job." Kate hurried out the front door, trying to lure Max away from the clerk and the curious onlookers in the lobby.

"I'm sorry." Max let out a deep breath and followed her, a look of confusion etched across his tanned face. "I'm acting like an idiot. But I wanted you to come, and I was afraid that you wouldn't."

"You were?" Kate's surprised response popped

out before she could stop it. Max led her to a low-slung black sports car and opened the door for her. He paused, a dark look of intensity reflected in his eyes.

"Why didn't you stay last night?"

"Because I never should have been there. Just as I shouldn't be here this morning."

"Why? Were you uncomfortable with my friends?"

His friends? Truthfully, she couldn't recall a single one of them. "No, it wasn't that. It's just that I've never been in a place like this, with a man like you. You overwhelm me and I—we—oh, Lordy, this is coming out all wrong. Just go on to your meeting and forget about me, Max Sorrenson."

He was leaning forward, with one arm against the car on either side of her, pinning her down. She was doing her best to say no to a man whose very nearness was scrambling her brain and turning all her logical thoughts into confusion.

"No. I've tried all those arguments. They don't work. I mean, I think that we have to consider all the possibilities before making a decision. A relationship with an employee is something that I've avoided in the past. And I'm still not entirely sure that it's wise."

"Then why?"

"Because—because—oh, hell, because I want you with me. Isn't that enough?"

"Yes," she said simply. She was rewarded with a smile of pleasure that made her want to hug him. But what she did instead was kiss him. It was a quick, spontaneous kiss, the kind that any friend might give another friend, even if Max's groan and intake of breath threatened the friendship right from the start.

"Great," he said, pulling back. "Now we'd better hurry, or I'm going to be late for my meeting."

"No, wait. Do we have five more minutes?"

"Sure, why?"

"I want to change my clothes."

"Okay, but I like the shirt. It's . . . awesome, or it will be once it gets wet."

Kate gave him a playful slap and ran down the walk. She tried not to imagine what the day would bring as she exchanged her bag lady outfit for trim white shorts, a clean Braves T-shirt, and a fresh pair of white sneakers. The baseball cap gave way to a perky visor, and she was back at the car before she had time to change her mind.

They were just two people, a guy and a girl, out for a day in the Florida sun. She'd leave it at that for now. No use anticipating trouble before it arrived, she decided.

Max watched Kate slide into the passenger seat, and then he started the engine. Throwing propriety to the winds, he flung back his head and let out one of his aunt's favorite expressions of approval. "Yahoo!"

He drove the sports car down the road beneath moss-draped trees, alongside squatty palms growing in gray-black dirt. Kate loved reading the names of the streets on the signs at the intersections of the narrow little sandy lanes that led off toward the water: Seagrove, Grayton, Blue Mountain Beach.

The sun was shining. The ocean breeze was tugging at Kate's hair like a lover sneaking secret kisses, and Max, watching Kate, couldn't stop smiling. Every time he stole a look at her, she was looking at him, and finally they both gave in and laughed out loud.

"What kind of car do you have, Kate?"

"Nothing like this, I'm afraid."

"Is it a sports car?"

"No, just a plain old Chevy."

"Perfect, we should have driven it."

"Why on earth would you want to trade this beautiful machine for my ratty car?"

"Because," he said as he turned down a gravel road toward the ocean, "it probably doesn't have bucket seats." Max brought the car to an abrupt stop at the private parking area adjacent to the Hidden Cove Yacht Club. He turned off the engine, reached across the gear box, and pulled Kate close.

"It also doesn't run," she whispered breathlessly.

Max groaned softly, twisting his head so that his mouth fit perfectly against hers. She'd known his kiss would be hot, hard, and demanding. What she hadn't known was that she would lose herself in its power.

He pulled back and nuzzled her cheek as he steadied his breathing.

"You may have to move your meeting here."

"Meeting! Oh, hell. We'd better get going. I'll get the cooler. You bring the blanket."

"Blanket?" Before she could open her door, he already had the cooler in one hand and a blanket draped over one arm.

"So, I'll bring them both. You just bring the dessert."

"Dessert?"

"You, Kathryn. Follow me. Remember, all work and no play makes Max dull." Max waited for Kate to get out of the car, placed a wickedly suggestive kiss on her forehead, and marched briskly onto the floating pier. Kate scrambled down the dock behind him.

"I don't really think that you're dull, Max," Kate

protested, her voice a little subdued as she realized that Max had called her Kathryn. She wasn't
sure why that bothered her, but it did. Kathryn
was another person, the mysterious woman from
Max's dinner party. She was Kate, and Kate had
her feet planted squarely on the ground.

"Neither did I," Max confessed over his shoulder, "but I'm beginning to think that Aunt Dorothea was right. Maybe the word is monotonous,
tedious, stodgy."

"Maybe the word is dormant."

"I think I like the idea of being awakened, Kate.
Let's get to the boat."

Gray and white gulls made shrill angry noises
as they streaked across the water at the dock's
edge. Kate glanced around, seeing for the first
time the fleet of assorted boats bobbing gently in
the cobalt blue water. Smartly dressed people were
climbing aboard various boats. They called their
greetings to Max, who seemed to know everyone.
The scene was bright and happy. Big fluffy clouds
ballooned across the sky in the bright sunshine.

Max's boat seemed much too large for one man
to sail. Kate swallowed a gasp as she read its
name: *Secret Lady*.

"Take this, Kate," Max said from the open area
leading down to what was apparently a sleeping
cabin. He handed her a bright orange life jacket.

"Slip it on like a vest and snap the catch," he
instructed as he fastened his own. "Every passenger on board the *Secret Lady* wears one."

Kate complied silently, allowing herself to examine his trim, tanned body as he emerged from the
compartment. He was wearing white sneakers,
crisp white shorts, and a dark pink polo shirt. He
looked like . . . like raspberry sherbert. And she'd
always had a weakness for raspberries.

Max seemed unaware of her scrutiny as he moved to the seat near the tiller and motioned for Kate to sit down beside him. He turned the key, and the churning sound of the boat's motor filled the strained silence. "We'll use the motor to move us out of the cove, into the bay, and out into deep water. Then the wind will power us."

Any thought Kate had of conversation died when the engine roared to life, and the boat moved slowly out of the cover. Soon they had left behind the gleaming white beaches with the charming names. Kate felt the tension drain away. When they were well out into the Gulf, Max killed the engine and began to unfurl the sails.

"First we hoist the mainsail, then the jib. Then we winch up the sails. That means pull them tight. We'll just trim them so they won't flutter, then we'll cleat them."

"Cleat them?" Kate asked.

"Fasten them down."

Kate marveled at his quick actions. She'd never seen anybody so competent, so sure of himself. There was no wasted motion in this man's life, no beat-up old Chevy, and no grand unknown waiting over the next horizon. If he did a thing, he did it well. If he wanted it, he got it. Every action he made was orderly and purposeful. Kate felt a warning twinge of doubt, pushed it aside, and concentrated on his words.

"Now we note the direction of the wind, check the current, take the helm, and we're off." Soon they were making a zigzag motion through the wind. The breeze became more powerful, and the boat seemed to leap across the dark, white-capped waves.

"You love it, don't you?" she finally said.

"Yes, I do. I can come out here and leave everything behind. Here there are no problems except an occasional squall, and they aren't man-made. I guess you'd call this my escape. How do you escape, Kate?"

"I take—no, I took—how-to classes. Lots of how-to classes. In five years' time, there wasn't anything I didn't learn about."

"But plumbing, mechanics, carpentry? I've never known a woman who liked getting dirty."

"I got into it by accident. I'd planned to go to college, but after my mother became ill, I had to forget about that. The only thing I could afford was cheap classes. And the only cheap classes were in the adult education programs in the local high schools."

"Why not study typing or cake decorating?"

"I tried some of those the first year. And then one quarter, I signed up late and the only thing left was cabinet-making. I decided, why not? And I found out that hammering and sawing was exactly what I needed. I worked out all my frustrations. And you know what? I'm good at it."

"Physical exertion. I can understand that. That's why I run."

I know, she almost said, *I watched you*. But the thought steered her mind into a direction she refused to allow herself to go.

She was glad that he'd asked her to come. She'd never sailed before, and she loved the feel of the spray on her face. He was right. Out on the water there were no problems. Everything seemed unimportant, and she was willing to let the wind take her wherever it chose. Overhead, wispy clouds had chased the cotton puffs away. She scanned the horizon, lifting her face to meet the warmth of the sun.

For a time Kate was successful in keeping her eyes averted from the man holding the helm. She'd never spent time with anyone before where the silence was pleasant. She liked that he didn't talk. Some men couldn't stand silence. Max was content to sit back and let her enjoy the moment without telling her that she should.

He'd unbuttoned his shirt as soon as they'd left the cove. Now he removed it entirely, revealing the total maleness of his upper body. Kate sucked in her breath and closed her eyes. In spite of the cool breeze, she was very warm.

"Are you hungry?"

"Starving," Kate admitted, hoping beyond hope that the peculiar feeling in the pit of her stomach would go away if she ate.

"So am I. If you'll go below, you'll find a thermos of coffee and a brown paper bag of doughnuts. Bring them up here, and we'll eat."

After a few faltering steps, Kate found her balance and located the thermos, the cups, and the doughnuts. She carried them to the deck and spread the feast out on the top of a built-in toolbox. She poured the steaming coffee, took a quick sip, and found to her delight that it was sweet.

"Hey, swabbie, I think I ought to explain that it is the duty of the crew to see that the captain is fed first."

"Sorry, Captain. I'm starving. I was out to dinner last night with a handsome man who interfered with my appetite." She reached across the seat and held out a cup and a doughnut.

"I can handle the wheel and the coffee. But the doughnut? You're either going to have to steer the boat or feed me. It's the law of the sea."

"If I don't, do I have to walk the plank?"

"No, you have to . . ." his voice dropped to a throaty rumble. "I think you'd better come over here and—" he meant to say "feed me," but instead said, "kiss me, Kate."

Kate slid across the seat until she was only inches away. Her breathing was shallow as she broke the sugary confection in half and held it up to Max's lips. He looked into Kate's eyes, and she knew that doughnuts were the last thing on Max's mind. He was hungry. She was hungry. But their hunger wasn't for food.

Max opened his mouth and took a bite of the doughnut, chewed it slowly, and parted his lips to lick off the sweet powder. He missed a sprinkling of sugar on his chin, and she reached out with one finger to wipe it away. Her fingertip rubbed against the faint stubble of his beard. Max seemed not to be breathing. He held himself motionless as the boat caught a quick, even breeze.

Kate jerked away. She slid down the bench, took a hurried sip from the cup she held in her left hand, and dropped her gaze to her feet.

That was a big mistake. When she looked down at her feet, she also could see Max's muscular legs. She imagined they were the kind of legs that could fit intimately around a woman's body. She blushed. How did a man and a woman ever spend normal time together? She was confused.

"Thank heaven you're not one of those women who thinks she'd explode if she ate a big fat greasy doughnut rolled in sugar. Though I must admit that from your Braves T-shirt, I'd guess you were more the hot dogs and mustard type."

Grateful to Max for the interruption, Kate glanced down at her shirt, then back at him. The hair on his chest looked as though it were frosted, and

Kate's shirt had a patch of white sugar on Chief Noc-A-Homa's headdress.

"I am a hot dog and mustard person. You know that wild story Dorothea told you about me was pure fabrication."

"Oh, I know. At least I know you're not some writer for a men's magazine. Dorothea confessed this morning. I already knew that you were a whiz with a pipe wrench. Helen told me you'd fixed the dryer. But are you really a baseball fan?"

"I am." She relaxed, adapting quickly to the lightness of the conversation. "Watched almost every game the Braves played."

"Went to a lot of them, did you?"

"In person? No, I didn't," she admitted sheepishly. "I watched on television, and only when I wasn't watching old movies and soap operas."

"Of course. Cesar and Lorenzo."

"You don't forget a thing, do you?" Kate said. "You must wonder about me. My mother was ill for quite a while, and we spent a lot of time watching television together. I guess it was emotional escapism, like your sailing. I know when I'm watching that the characters and the stories aren't true. I don't have to solve their problems, or assume the responsibility for their actions. And when the show is over, my troubles seem unimportant."

"That doesn't explain Cesar and Lorenzo."

"Well, mother and I worked out a kind of shorthand. I mean, it was hard for her to talk, to explain her feelings. So, if somebody put on airs, pretended to be someone he wasn't, he became Rich Little."

"I see."

"If somebody was really hokey, he or she was Ma or Pa Kettle. If my mother had a bad day it became a *Dark Victory* day. I'm afraid that I got into the habit of identifying concepts with characters."

"And Lorenzo and Cesar?" Max smiled his wicked smile and waited. He wasn't going to let go.

"All right, I called you that partly because you're wealthy, and partly because you're a . . ."

"Hunk?"

"I can't believe I said that. Of course, I also can't believe you've never watched that television program."

"Oh, from now on I intend to," Max said with a wink, as he remembered the new television already installed in his bedroom. "Popcorn, soft drinks, the works. Next Friday night. Want to join me?"

"Popcorn," she said softly. "My mother liked popcorn with lots of butter and salt."

Max sensed the change in her, the return of the tension that had vanished in the sun. And he knew that she had her private demons too. Only she hid them behind a bright approach to life. He wanted to throw the anchor overboard and comfort her in his arms.

"That must have been hard for you, caring for someone who was ill."

"Hard?" Kate was saying. "Caring for someone you love? Never. My mother was a wonderful person. She was never a hardship. She spent her life caring for me. It was only fair that I give back that kind of love. I had help from friends and neighbors. I went to school, had a job working for a florist for a few years until . . . Oh, what's that?"

Kate could suddenly see the brightly colored resort area in the distance. The sight of the coastline brought their conversation to a close. The building that caught her attention belonged to a competitor, Max explained. He pointed out with pride several other properties that belonged to Sorrenson Properties, Inc.

"The buildings are very beautiful," Kate said softly.

"Thirty miles of the most beautiful beaches in the world, and I intend to keep them just as they are now, for families to enjoy and so that the local residents can live a good life. Nobody is going to spoil my part of the world, if I can prevent it."

Something about his determination caught Kate's attention. "Is something really threatening this paradise?"

"Even the Garden of Eden had a snake. Our snake has two heads, gambling and drug trafficking. South Florida is already in trouble, and we're next. Outsiders are buying up the properties and introducing gambling. That way they can launder drug money. Here on the Carnival Strip, we've formed an association of property owners who have agreed not to sell to outsiders without allowing the association first option."

"Can you enforce it?"

"Well, not legally. So far we're operating under a gentlemen's agreement. But right now we've committed all our funds. Once we sell something we've bought to our own hand-picked owner, we'll replenish our funds. Until that happens, I'm worried."

"Sounds risky to me."

"It is. We never buy the property in the association's name. We just buy an option. Then, very discreetly, we find a suitable buyer and transfer the option. The building is never officially for sale."

"Do you think that gambling and drugs go together?"

"I know they do. By keeping out the gamblers, we cut off the monster's head."

"But that doesn't stop the man on the street, does it?"

"No, nor the woman either, but it's a start."

"My mother was on morphine, heavy doses of morphine," Kate said. "She hated to take drugs, even the legal ones. The medication turned her into a zombie, but at least she wasn't in pain."

"My mother took drugs to stop hurting too. Illegal drugs. And they killed her."

"Oh, Max. I'm sorry."

"It's all right. I never knew her. She died when I was five years old. I barely remember her. Went for a swim, the newspaper report said. I was twelve when I heard the gossip. Matthew told me the truth. She couldn't get off the stuff, and she killed herself. You know, I've never told that to anybody else until now."

"Thank you, Max. I know it isn't easy to talk about those things. Opening up is risky. I understand about risks."

"And you're a risk-taker. But I'm not, or I never have been in the past."

"That's the only way you know that you're alive, Max."

"Perhaps, but avoiding risks is the way you keep life under control. Control was always important to me," he said, wanting to add "before you came along."

Max was moving the boat toward a break in the land. "We'll cut through here into Saint Andrews Bay and across to Panama City." In a very short time he was securing the sails and starting the engine to position them at the dock.

Kate removed her life jacket while Max was pulling on his shirt. She reluctantly followed him up the walkway and into the cool darkness of the Sea Sands Yacht Club. The trip had been nice. Talking had been nice. But now they were on dry land and the curious glances of the early lunch crowd hastened her walk. She was horrified when Max stopped at the restaurant entrance and took her hands.

"Kate, I've arranged to meet the Hotel Association committee here. Would you like to join us, or would you rather walk down the pier? There are some interesting craft booths along with the fish vendors."

"The pier," she agreed quickly, grateful for an escape. "I wouldn't feel right about intruding on your meeting. What would your associates think?"

"Kate, there's one other thing you need to know about me. I don't care what people think about what I do. As long as I'm satisfied, the world can take a flying leap."

"That's great, Max, but I'd rather wander around, if you don't mind."

"Fine. I'll be about an hour, and then I'll start down the pier looking for you. Kate . . ."

Max dropped her hands and lifted her chin with his fingertips. "Kate, don't run away. Promise?"

She didn't know that he was going to kiss her until he did. She didn't know that she was going to let him until she did. She wasn't sure it had really happened as she watched him turn and head into the restaurant with an uncharacteristically jaunty walk. He was actually whistling.

She was halfway out the door before she realized that the tune Max was whistling was "Some Enchanted Evening."

And the evening was yet to come.

•   •   •

Kate meandered down the beach front shopping area with the charming but inaccurate name "the pier." There were shops featuring shells made into everything from jewelry to night-lights. The Beachcombers featured hemp hammocks and wall hangings. She found one delightful art shop displaying some of Matthew Blue's paintings.

"He's one of our local artists," the shop owner explained. "Came here as a boy on a freighter, the story goes, and eventually he owned one of the largest fleets of fishing boats around. Everything he touches seems to turn to gold. Just look at the price tag on those paintings."

Kate moved closer to the painting of a wistful boy watching the fleet of boats disappearing over the horizon. The child looked suspiciously like Max. The price tag, she discovered with surprise, might have applied to Max too. Matthew had to be doing very well.

It was noon now, and the sun beat down relentlessly, burning her bare arms and legs. With the ocean breeze blocked by the buildings, perspiration ran down her body, and her skin started to turn pink.

Maybe wearing long pants would have been smart, she thought. Max hadn't seemed to object to her Ellie Mae Clampett look. She definitely didn't object to his raspberry sherbert attire, she mused, and licked her dry lips. Kate closed her eyes, trying to blot out the very real picture that had appeared in her mind, the picture of a man with thick dark hair and black eyes. She opened them again. He was still there. He really was there, running down the pier, straight toward her.

"Kate!" He caught her in his arms and swung

her around. "What about it, are you ready for our grand adventure?"

Was she ready? Did a cool icy drink look interesting to the last legionnaire to cross the desert? Max was holding her, his arms loosely hooked about her waist. A fresh wave of heat washed over her, yet this time they were standing in the shade.

"Sure."

He swung her around again. "All work and no play, remember?"

"I thought they were one and the same to you, so how can I tell?" Kate gave in to the urge she'd had all day and leaned against him.

"You'll be able to tell," Max said with a laugh. "When I work, I'm very, very good, and when I play, I'm irresistible."

"Which are you doing now?" She leaned back into his arms and looked up into his face. *Tilt! Tilt!* Her senses screamed as the other shoppers faded away into the sunshine. She was waiting, waiting for him to kiss her. And he didn't disappoint her.

Max brushed his lips across her face, beginning above her left eyebrow and working his way down to her mouth. Her lips parted naturally beneath his, and what had started as a playful hello became an intimate exchange of desire. A wolf whistle, followed by clapping hands shocked them back to reality. He slid his arm up to her shoulder and turned her around, clasping her hand.

"This has to be 'playing,' darling," he said, grinning foolishly. "Let's get out of here."

"You got one thing right," she said as she broke into a run to keep up with his long stride. "It was irresistible. Where are we going?"

"Back to the boat, Kate. We have a picnic to get to, and I'd like a swim, wouldn't you?"

Only if it's at the North Pole, she thought. "Food. Great. I'm starving," Kate agreed, with a light laugh. "Where are we going to have this lunch?"

"There's a small island down the coast. It's very private. We'll have our picnic there."

They made their way back to the dock quickly. Max started the boat moving back out into the Gulf, and soon they were flying across the water.

The sea breeze was wonderful. Kate pulled the hem of her T-shirt up under the life jacket and savored the feel of the wind against her damp skin. Soon she could see a patch of white and green looming up ahead. They hadn't spoken, and Kate was glad. But the force of Max's dark gaze made her constantly aware of his presence.

"Come over here."

Kate jumped with the guilty feeling that he could somehow read her thoughts.

". . . and hold this steady, like so," he commanded, "while I lower the sail."

They were nearing land, and the brisk breeze was threatening to take them away. Kate managed to slip by him and take the helm. Max strapped the canvas down and dropped the heavy iron anchor overboard. Kate looked skeptically at the beach, still a distance away.

"And how do we get the food to shore, or do you walk on water too?"

"I don't, and we don't. Not just yet," Max answered, removing his life vest. He gathered up the hem of his knit shirt and pulled it lazily over his head. "First we're going to have a real deep-water swim in the lagoon."

Max began to unzip his shorts and slide them down his muscular legs. He was wearing *the* suit, she realized, the same skimpy black suit he'd been wearing that morning in the elevator.

Kate knew she was staring. Just being near him all day had been emotionally draining. The touching and the kissing had pulled the tension between them to a fine thread, which threatened to break at any moment. Seeing Max's body now was more than she could stand.

"Well?" he demanded, arms crossed. "Are you going to join me?"

"Eh, no. I'm not going in," she said, feigning an interest in the clear turquoise blue water where they were anchored.

"What's the matter, wasn't swimming one of your how-to classes?"

"I didn't bring a suit."

"No problem. I always have a couple of extras in the cabin. Take your pick."

"No," she insisted. "I'd rather not, but you go ahead. I'll just watch." She felt the boat shift as he moved toward her.

Kate raised her eyes and her breath left her in a rush as she leaned away from him. He lifted her easily.

"What are you going to do?" Her voice came out in a gravelly whisper. She reached up, clutching his neck in an awkward motion to steady herself. She quickly realized her error. In clasping her arms about him, she had simply pulled herself closer, and now the feel of his body against her brought a new and equally alarming reaction. "You don't want to throw me in, do you?"

"No," he said in a voice that had deepened measurably, "that's not what I want to do at all. But I think we're both overheated and need cooling off."

Max walked to the side, gave her a quick kiss, and dropped her unceremoniously over the side. The cool slap of water was first a shock, then was a heavenly relief to Kate's parched body. She came up treading water. A powerful echoing spray of water told Kate that Max had joined her. She closed her eyes and dipped her head back, allowing the flow of water to wash her hair back from her face.

"Isn't that better? Sorry you lost your glasses. Now you need to lose those cumbersome clothes." He paddled lazily toward her.

"Glasses? And my visor. I lost my visor." Kate began to whirl around, searching frantically. She felt exposed, as though she had been unmasked.

She'd known that coming with Max was risky. Now it was put-up-or-shut-up time, and she didn't know what to do. He was right. Her clothing was in the way. But take it off?

Kate panicked. She started swimming toward shore, her anxiety transforming itself into untapped energy. She didn't try to analyze her wild flight from the man in the penthouse suite. She just needed to get away. By the time her knees bumped the sandy bottom at the island edge, Kate heard the sound of the boat's motor close behind her. She'd reached the shore, but she hadn't escaped.

"I should have known," she muttered, and flung herself on the beach. *"Fantasy Island."*

Five

"Kate! Kate! Are you all right?"

Kate lay face down on the sand, eyes closed, heart pounding as she tried to pull air into lungs heaving from exertion. She heard the boat's motor die, followed by a thud as the bow of the boat was beached on the sand.

While she lay very still, Kate tried desperately to marshal some line of defense against the man splashing toward her through the shallow water. Once they'd left the hotel, she had known he would make love to her. And she'd thought she was ready. But he'd let down some of his barriers, and she'd learned that he was more than just a powerful, handsome man. Now she was afraid. How could she stop him from getting to close to her? How could she stop herself from wanting him too much?

"Kate, what happened?" Max dropped down beside her and turned her over. She was breathing.

He could see the rise and fall of her chest. But she wasn't answering. "Open your eyes, Kate, darling."

Nothing.

"Well, Max, drastic measures seem to be needed," he said aloud. "This woman may be the most beautiful castaway on the Gulf Coast, but she's in trouble. CPR. You've never performed it, but you know the procedure. First make certain that the throat passageway isn't obstructed." He leaned forward.

Kate's eyes flew open. "No. I mean, that isn't necessary. I'm all right."

"As the captain, I'm responsible for the members of my crew. I'd better be sure. Let me check your pulse." He made an elaborate pretense of finding the pulse point in her neck.

His technique felt more like a caress than a medical procedure, and Kate held her breath.

"Ah, a bit rapid, I think. Better check the heartbeat." Solemnly Max laid his head across her breast and listened.

If her pulse had been erratic before, it was playing pinball inside her now. "Get off of me, Max. What are you trying to do, smother me to death?"

The concern on his face changed into a smile as he raised up and began to laugh. "I thought I was about to perform artificial respiration on a dying woman. I guess I was wrong. Too bad I didn't get to the part where I massaged her chest."

"From where I am, I think you did—massage my chest, that is." Kate rubbed her cheek, dislodging a layer of white powder from her face. She took a deep breath, came to her knees, and looked down at her gritty clothes.

"Yuck! This isn't sand, this is a new kind of glue I've fallen into. If your Aunt Dorothea could see me now, she'd say I was a writer for the *Sewer Workers Daily* and that you're addlebrained for asking me to come along."

Max made a move to reach down and lift her up. "Here, let me help."

"No thanks. I can manage." She stood and moved stiffly back into the water toward the boat.

"What are you doing now?"

"What I should have done in the beginning. Getting out of these clothes."

"At last a sensible idea. Do you need any help?'

"Not on your life, bossman. You just pull up a turtle shell and wait."

Neither of the swimsuits on board offered much more covering that the suit Max was wearing. But turnabout was fair play. And play was the name of the game on Fantasy Island.

Kate jerked her wet clothes off and tied the scanty triangles of knit fabric about her hips and around her neck. She'd never sailed to a tropical paradise before, and she might never have such a day again. Somewhere between the shore and the swimsuit, she'd decided that she was going to enjoy herself.

Perhaps Dorothea was right. Perhaps she could be whomever she wanted to be. She could live in the present and fantasize about her future. *All there is*, she thought, waist-deep in the crystal blue waters, *is now*.

She moved into the deeper water, submerged herself, and sluiced the sand from her hair, before moving toward the beach and the wide-eyed man who was watching her.

"You're wrong," Max said. "I may have thrown overboard a writer for the *Sewer Workers Daily*, but this is Kathryn, an almond-eyed nymph from the sea, that I'm looking at now." He started toward her.

The wet suit clung to her body, concealing little. Though she had been just as intriguing in the coveralls the first day he'd seen her, he hadn't realized how delicate she was. Wielding that wrench in the bathroom, she'd seemed bigger.

They stood only inches apart, swaying in the surf, bodies frosted with mist blown from the sea. Even the cool water couldn't quench the flame that leapt from Kate to Max and back again.

"Not smart, bossman," she said with a dare in her voice. "Sea nymphs capture their lovers, imprison them in seashells, and wear them around their necks on chains of seaweed."

"Lucky shell," Max said hoarsely, his eyes drawn to the space between her breasts.

"Lucky nymph."

As she looked up at him, he felt something wonderful happen. The warmth in his chest heated the very air he was breathing. She wasn't laughing anymore. She was waiting for him to take her in his arms and kiss her. He leaned down, capturing her lips with his. Their kiss started slowly, intensified, and changed into a wild, hot frenzy of release.

"We ought to get some sunscreen on you before you burn," Max said as he caught his breath between kisses.

"Too late," she said with a gasp, feeling his lips nudge away the top of her bathing suit. "We're already on fire."

Max untied the knot behind Kate's neck and

those at the sides of the suit. He stripped off his own suit, and they were both nude. There was no time for wondering, no questions, no answers. He lifted her into his arms and laid her back on the warm sand as though the beach were an altar and she were a mystical virgin.

As Max began to worship her with his lips and hands, Kate felt sunbursts explode everywhere he touched. She couldn't tell where she ended and Max began. The tiny flame that had begun to glow when she'd first seen him in the mirror now erupted into a raging passion. She let out a sob of yearning as she felt herself engulfed by liquid fire.

When at last he lowered his muscular body over hers, Kate melted into him, losing herself completely to the relentless waves of desire that built into a final thunderous explosion.

Afterward, Max lay across her for a moment, then raised himself up and kissed her. "You look as if you've been sprinkled with sugar."

"I feel more like melted honey."

The raging storm that had taken them had been quick and violent. That was the way Kate wanted it, without the gentle promise of love. She'd been on fire, and their coming together had been the release of violent emotion. Now they were calm, and the regular pulsing of the incoming tide lapped a lullaby gently across their feet.

"You really are going to burn," Max said. "Your skin, I mean. It's so fair." He came to his feet, bringing her along with him. The experience had rocked him as well, and he reverted for a moment to the old Max, the Max who had never known such awareness of a woman's feelings.

"You mean I'm going to freckle."

"I like your freckles, Kate Weston. They're honest and open, just as you are. I like you, too. But I think we'd better wash off this sand and get that sunscreen before you blister in places you can't leave uncovered."

"Covered? Max, our clothes!"

Max glanced around. The clothes were definitely gone. He laughed. "Well, it looks as if we've gone back to nature in the most basic way."

"Not on your life, Robinson Crusoe. To the boat!" Kate started into the water.

Max groaned in exaggerated remorse. "Shucks! And I was looking forward to dressing ourselves in fig leaves."

Inside the cramped cabin, Kate tried to avoid touching Max as she rummaged around for replacement garments. She took the swimsuit he offered her and fastened the top around her neck.

"Ahhhh!" He groaned as if he were in deep pain.

"What's wrong?" Kate turned in alarm.

"I seem to have a problem, Kate."

Kate glanced down at his hands, the hands that were trying to force a very small spandex swimsuit over a body that was refusing to cooperate.

"It won't fit, Kate. You've ruined me forever. I may never be able to wear clothes again. I'll have to stay indoors, wear raincoats, and take cold showers."

Kate was trembling all over. For the first time in her life she couldn't think. As he took her into his arms, she moaned. His lips brushed over her still-swollen breasts. His unexpected arousal pushed against her, making her mindless with need. She suddenly realized they were on the small bunk.

He was kissing her, touching her, entering her once again. She gave herself over to sensation, knowing that she might never experience the wonder of such a happening again.

They dressed silently afterward, each stunned by the intensity of their coming together. Max pulled her back into the water, and they played at washing each other until they were clean and the sense of awkwardness between them was gone.

"Come with me, woman. I'm going to cover you with lotion." He led her back under the edge of a stand of tall majestic pines, where he had spread the blanket beside the plastic cooler.

"Sure," she said, and laughed, no longer trying to separate herself from the island god she'd conjured up in her most erotic daydream. "Annette Funicello and Frankie Avalon." She lay down on her stomach and folded her arms beneath her forehead. "Okay, have at it, Frankie," she said. "Surf's up."

"Frankie Avalon? Kate, don't you watch any current programs on television?"

Max poured sunscreen into his palm and began to rub it across her back.

"There was a time when I didn't. But I don't watch television now. There are too many things I haven't done yet. That's why I don't understand a man who knows exactly where he's going. I'd rather be surprised. Tell the truth now, wouldn't you?"

"Surprised? I'd say that my life has taken on a definite quality of the unknown. Just look at me. I'm out here on a deserted island in the middle of the afternoon without a care in the world. You're a very special lady, Kate."

"Nothing special about me, Max. I'm pretty ordinary, except for what I do for a living. And if I were a man, I'd be even duller."

"I don't want to talk about work, Kate. I want to know about you. Tell me about your family."

Kate took a deep breath. "Okay, bossman. Here it is. I never knew my father. He came from a wealthy family. My mother got pregnant. He hit the road. I was born. She went back home, settled down and became the best waitress at Sam's Diner in Pikeville, Kentucky. There wasn't a lot to do in Pikeville then, and not much more now. It's just normal, small-town America."

"Why didn't you leave?"

"I planned to. I'd just graduated from high school and enrolled in junior college when we found out that my mother had cancer. I had to go to work. We needed the money. Then came her surgery, chemotherapy, the works."

His hands had left her back and were working their way down her thighs. Her skin was beginning to be very warm, and she wasn't at all sure that the heat was coming from the sun. She forced herself to continue. As long as she was thinking about her mother, she couldn't think about Max's hands.

"The television was her window to the outside world. But she didn't like current programs very much. Old movies weren't threatening to her. She loved the past. It was safe and happy. The bad guys were obvious, and the good guys always won. I think that's about it. A lot different from your background, I'll bet."

"Maybe and maybe not, since I never knew my father either. And we didn't have a television." His hands skimmed down the backs of her legs. "Turn over."

"Why?"

"Because I'm committing your body to memory, and I'm ready to catalog the rest of you," he said with exaggerated patience. "Because you need this sunscreen on both sides if you're planning to do any work tomorrow."

"If I'm planning to do any work tomorrow? Of course I'm planning to work tomorrow, if I don't get fired again."

"I'm not going to fire you. Life without you would be much too dull. You need a job, and I need to change my life-style, remember?"

Kate was finding it hard to remember why anybody had ever thought Max was dull. A little stern maybe, but she was beginning to understand that quality in him. Compassionate? Romantic? Caring? Sexy? He was all those and more. Without even thinking, she turned over.

Max poured a dollop of lotion on Kate's stomach and swallowed hard. He began to rub the clear liquid over her shoulders, making quick feathery motions across her collarbone and down the sides of her breasts to her abdomen. Up and down, faster, slower. The muscles in his neck were corded tight.

Kate forced herself to open her eyes. "Max?"

His eyes were glazed. He smiled provocatively.

Kate tried to remain coolheaded and detached. Her skin was on fire, and it wasn't due to the sun.

Max could see her breathing become shallow. Beneath the skimpy swimsuit top, her nipples had peaked into tight cherries, begging him to take them in his mouth. He could feel his own body harden and thrust against her thigh.

"Kate?" His voice was hoarse with desire.

"I don't understand. Why do you want me, Max?"

"I don't know, Kate. Must there be answers?"

He leaned down and took her nipple in his mouth. As he touched her he felt the passion between them build quickly to the point of no return. It intensified, gathered force, and swept them away with its power.

"Max!" Half beneath him, Kate twisted to allow the other nipple the pleasure of his kiss.

This time he seemed to move in slow motion as his mouth left her breasts and captured her lips again. She burned with the need to touch the man beside her. She thrust her hands through his hair, slid them down his neck, across his chest, and lower, until she was holding his hardness in her hand. She heard him gasp, and she gloried in the power she held over him.

They were engulfed by a slow-moving tidal wave of sensation that burned the very sand beneath the blanket where they lay. Finally he lifted himself over her and they came together, racing toward the sun, experiencing wave after wave of exquisite pleasure until at last they were spent.

"The world may never know, Max, but between you and me, never let the word 'dull' be mentioned again."

"Ah, Kate, my Kate." He moved back to her side. Lifting himself on one elbow, he kissed her lips gently.

His kiss was almost spiritual. Kate let out a deep, satisfied sigh.

"Kate. Do you have any notion of what I feel? I think that I'm beginning to care for you, Kate Weston, very much. I think we may have to extend your contract. I don't think I'm going to be able to let you go."

She lay listening to his unsteady breathing. In all her wishes for adventure, she'd never pictured herself making love to such a man on a deserted island. She'd never known that a man and woman could come together in such an explosion of desire. A week ago she would never have believed that she'd share this kind of bond with this kind of man. Now? Was it all a fantasy? It had to be.

"Did you hear me, Kate?" Max's hand was lying across her stomach, his fingers splayed like a steel fan, holding her still.

"Don't say things you don't mean, Max. Don't care too much. You mustn't feel that way about me. This isn't part of any movie. I know that you've learned the right lines, but I don't need to hear you say them. I understand."

"I don't know what you mean. Script? If you think that this is some kind of play acting, you're wrong." He removed his hand from Kate's stomach and sat up.

"No, you're just caught up in the fantasy, too. Hey!" She twisted away and stood. "Bossman, let's get to the food. You promised me a picnic. I never get serious on an empty stomach."

Max stared at her in amazement, a situation in which he continually found himself. The woman was completely bewildering. They'd just made love, magnificent love. He'd opened up to Kate as he'd never done to any other woman, and suddenly she was pulling away from him.

"Dammit, Kate. What does that mean?"

"It means that this isn't real, Max. You and I, here on this island, making love on the beach. This isn't real. I understand that. When we get back to the hotel—that's real."

Max let out an angry sigh and shook his head. "You mean this is all some kind of pretend trip for you? It's a fantasy? Well, it means much more to me, and I won't deny that. I'll drop it for now, Kate, because I know you feel something for me, even if you won't admit it. Why don't we have lunch?"

Kate let the subject drop and watched as Max uncovered the food.

The sail back to the hotel was much too short. Max didn't make any more provocative statements about how he felt, making it easy for her to pretend that they were just a regular guy and his girl returning from a nice Sunday outing. Outside her room, Kate lost all awareness of time as Max kissed her good-bye.

"Kate?" he whispered.

"Max, what are you doing?"

"I'm touching you, Kate. I like touching you." He slid one hand beneath her shirt and cupped her breast. The other hand slipped down and cupped her bottom, lifting her hard against him.

"May I come in, Kate? Please? I don't want to leave you."

Earlier he'd been demanding. Now he was asking politely. This unexpected tenderness was part of the new Max, and she didn't know how to respond. She sighed and lifted her hand to run it along the edge of his lip.

"You want to stay here, in the employees' quarters? Wouldn't you be a little out of place?"

"If you're here, it will be the Taj Mahal."

"I'm on call tonight, Max. And I don't think it would be a good idea for you to stay."

"I know," he whispered, "but I understand that there's an Atlanta Braves game on TV, and I thought we'd watch it."

She tried to move away from the intimacy that was turning her body into Silly Putty. "I don't think we'd get much watching done here."

"All right, let's go for a walk. I know a little spot down the beach that's secluded and . . ."

It took every ounce of control Kate could muster to twist out of his grasp. She would have been content to spend the night, the next month, the next year in Max's arm. But she couldn't.

"No, Max. Too much has happened too fast. You have to go. I can't think while you're touching me. Maybe tomorrow."

"No, not tomorrow, Kate." He pulled her close and kissed her again and again before drawing back. "I have to leave for New York on the red-eye flight. Come with me."

"To New York? Now, would that be an idea. Work two days and run away with the boss. I can't, Max. Be practical. You go to New York, and when you get back, we'll see."

With a sigh of resignation, Max pulled his hand from under her shirt. He lifted his head and looked down at her in confusion. "Are you sure?"

No, she wanted to say. The only thing she was sure of was that when she found her place in the sun, she didn't expect to get burned by its heat.

"No, I'm not sure of anything, Max. But I think you need to go." Kate knew that she was hurting him, but she didn't know what else to say.

"All right, Kate." He drew himself up and stepped back. "I'll see you when I get back."

After one last quick, sweet kiss, he was gone.

Kate went inside and closed the door.

Damn Ricardo Montalban. She wish she'd never watched *Fantasy Island.* She'd made up her mind to let Max make love to her, but she didn't know how to handle this kind of relationship. Adventure she craved, but never in her wildest imagination had she equated conquering new horizons with romance. One thing she did know, she hadn't imagined the way Max Sorrenson made her feel.

Max leaned back against the brocaded airplane seat and flexed his tired neck muscles. For the first time, he'd lost his intense power of concentration. In the middle of an earnest presentation at the board meeting, the memory of a pair of warm brown eyes had intruded, and he'd suddenly been back on the beach being kissed by a woman who called him bossman and ordered him around.

Max leaned his head back and closed his eyes, wondering what he was going to do about Kate. They'd made fierce, intense love, but when he'd given voice to his feelings, she'd drawn back. They had both been surprised by the pure physical reaction they'd experienced. They'd eaten lunch and talked. But he'd sensed her uncertainty.

Max hadn't wanted to leave the Carnival Strip the next day. His scheduled trip to New York for the board meeting was one he'd have bypassed if he'd had time to prepare anyone else. Then before the board meeting had ended he'd received the urgent call from fellow hotel owner, Red Garden. Red had been made an offer for his newly completed hotel, the Showboat. The property hadn't even been on the market, but the offer was just too good for him to turn down.

"Dammit, Red, can't you give the Hotel Association a few days to make a counteroffer?" Max had argued. "You've barely got the place open. I need to get back to my office to see if I can find a fairy godmother with a magic wand somewhere. Right now, I can't even think."

Red didn't know that what Max really wanted to get back to was Kate. Max couldn't concentrate on any problem until he'd seen Kate again.

"Sorry, Max. My buyer is anxious for a quick sale. I didn't intend to sell just now, but what can I do? I can't pass on this. You're the wonder boy. You've always come through before. Give me a higher bid, and it's yours."

Max had made the only offer he could, based on the funds available, and it hadn't been enough. For the first time, he couldn't come up with an answer.

The Hotel Association had turned into a kind of Chamber of Commerce. They'd committed some of their funds to mediate the fight between the local fishermen and the outsiders moving in. But the real problem was that the Association had not yet had time to replenish their funds since they'd bought the Oasis Hotel.

"Dammit, Red," Max had to admit, "we're close, but that's the best I can do. What about it?"

"I'm really sorry, Max. Their offer isn't that much higher, but I'll have to take it. Of course, we still have to wait for the mortgage holder to agree to the sale, so I'll be able to stall the signing until you get back. That's all I can promise."

Max had cut short his meeting and caught the next plane back to Panama City. Red would throw the traditional party to introduce the new owner to the Association, so at least he would get to meet the buyer. Though Max didn't know what good that would do.

The offer had appeared unexpectedly, at a time when Max was away, so that he couldn't keep a finger on the activities on the Strip. The entire deal must have happened fast and undercover. Max didn't like it—not at all. If he hadn't been so involved with Kate, he might have known more.

Kate. Even now she filled his thoughts. At the airport bookstand on the way out of New York Max had picked up a book called *Television and Movies Today*, a complete line-up of profiles on the stars. For the rest of his flight, he managed to keep his mind off Kate by studying the anthology of actors. With any luck he'd be able to pull a few stars out of the hat to match Kate's repertoire.

On board the plane, Max began to question his wisdom in ordering roses sent to Kate. They might have embarrassed her, flowers from the boss. He'd have done better to come up with something more warmhearted, like the corsage Andy Hardy took his date, Polly, for the senior prom. The odd-looking sailor costume Shirley Temple was wearing in the chapter about child stars reminded Max of the boat festival being held Sunday morning in the bay. Kate would love seeing the charter boats parade through the harbor for the Blessing of the Fleet.

When he deplaned at Panama City's airport, he phoned the hotel florist shop and ordered more flowers, this time daisies, lilies, snapdragons, and baby's breath. On the card he wrote:

I want to take you to the Blessing of the Fleet tomorrow morning. We'll have break-fast and watch the sun rise.

Max

P.S. Do I really look like Lorenzo Lamas?

Wow!

Kate tied her hair back and wiped her face before turning to her maintenance cart. For two nights she hadn't slept well, and she was uncharacteristically tired. Thank goodness Max was still out of town. At least she didn't have to face him yet. She'd thought that with time she'd be able to find an answer to the impossibility of a romance between a maintenance worker and the man at the top. She hadn't.

The long-stem roses he'd sent had been a complete surprise. She'd been thrilled and a bit embarrassed, knowing that the staff must be wondering about their relationship. The staff wasn't alone. She felt as if her insides were doing push-ups. Every so often, without warning, she lapsed into some kind of flashback of Max.

Max Sorrenson was a permanent part of the Carnival Strip, and she was a gypsy. After another week and a half, she'd take her paycheck, repair the car, and be gone. That was the sensible thing to do, and Max of all people would appreciate her being sensible.

Why, then, was being sensible so hard for her? She'd already learned that her intentions of doing the practical thing flew right out the window when Max touched her.

Gradually over the last few days she'd come to the conclusion that this had to be a case of opposites being attracted to each other. Max would have figured that out by the time he returned, and they'd go back to where they'd started.

Just as she was beginning to get herself together, the second bouquet came and sent her into orbit again. Time and distance obviously wasn't the answer. She didn't have an answer. Fortunately, she had three television sets to check and all the air-conditioning units on the fourth floor. Somehow she'd get through it. It was after lunch when the beeper attached to her belt went off. She dialed the desk.

"Kate, we have a problem."

Six

"Can you drop everything and go down to three-twenty-six?" Helen Stevens's voice was frantic. "It's Jody, one of the kids helping out for the summer. I can't make any sense out of what he said."

"As long as it doesn't involve water," Kate said, thinking about the problems she'd been involved in so far.

"I don't think so. He's babbling something about Mrs. Wilson's birdcage."

Kate quickly agreed to check on the situation. Making one last adjustment to the television set she was working on, Kate replaced its panel and took the stairs one flight down to the third floor. When she opened the door to room 326, she gasped in horror. A vacuum cleaner lay open on the floor. The bed was covered with a murky mound of purple-gray soot. Dust motes swirled through the air as Jody pawed through the heap, throwing debris everywhere like a dog digging for a bone.

"Goodness. What are you doing, Jody?" Kate

recognized the youngster as the high school student who normally worked around the pool.

"Kate, I think I'm in big time trouble. Pleeeeez! Help me. Like I've got to find it, or I'm out of here."

"Find what?" Kate held her breath and moved closer to the bed, eyeing Jody's frantic action. "Are you looking for buried treasure or digging a foxhole?"

"I'm looking for Mrs. Wilson's canary."

"Her canary? You mean there's a bird in the middle of all that muck?" Kate quickly dug in beside Jody. Between the two of them they raised a dust cloud that would have triggered a pollution alert. And then she heard it, a pitiful sound, not from the muck on the bed but from somewhere behind them. She glanced around, "Jody, it's up there."

The bird had apparently managed to free itself from the emptied bag of dust while Jody had been on the phone. It was now tottering precariously on the edge of the wall mirror.

"Wow!" Jody grabbed for the small mound of moldy feathers, which panicked and flew. The bird fluttered toward the door just as it opened.

"Hey, Kate, I'm saved! It's alive."

The bird flitted erratically toward the opening.

"Oh no! Close the door, dude. Don't let it escape!"

"Dude?"

The door slammed.

The distinctive masculine voice left no doubt as to who the "dude" in the doorway was.

Max was back.

Everything went into slow motion. Jody threw a towel at the canary, but missed the bird. The towel draped over Max's head. The bird whirled and darted toward the window. This time Kate snared it with a washcloth and dropped it into her uniform pocket. She looked up to see Max holding the towel in his hand. Jody was probably looking at time in the Big House. Maybe life.

"I hate to ask," Max said.

She was wrong. Max's voice was trembling with controlled amusement.

"Are you two talking about a major jailbreak, or do we just need a visit from the exterminator?"

"Neither, Mr. Sorrenson," Kate said quietly, trying to still the panic of the tiny creature she was holding. "Just a little accident. Mrs. Wilson's canary escaped."

"I see. It set off a smoke bomb to escape detection?"

Max could have dropped the stern employer act, but before Jody he'd automatically reverted. Now he was standing there worrying about a bird, when all he wanted to do was take Kate in his arms. He suddenly glared at Kate, the last thing he'd intended to do.

Kate couldn't decide whether he was angry or just going through the motions because Jody was present. He would have to find her at her worst. If her face looked like Jody's, they were both a charcoal color. No doubt she looked like a refugee from the garbage dump. Then she caught sight of a tiny quiver at the corner of his mouth, and she didn't care. All she wanted to do was kiss Max senseless.

Max hadn't thought far enough ahead to know what he would do when he got back. He'd justified his abrupt departure from New York by saying he had to get back to check on the sale of the Showboat and he'd finish his work on the way.

Yet, from the time he'd boarded the Florida-bound plane, he hadn't even opened his briefcase.

From the airport, he'd taken a taxi to the hotel and had cornered Helen Stevens at the front desk. He fabricated some ridiculous story about uniform sizes to ferret out Kate's location. Now he'd found her, and she wasn't alone. He gritted his teeth and tried to restrain himself from jerking her away from the pile of whatever that gray stuff was and stripping that uniform from her body so that he could touch her.

"It's my fault, sir," Jody said stepping forward valiantly, his young voice wavering as he tried in vain to control its high pitch. "Mrs. Wilson asked me to clean her bird cage."

"I see. One small canary caused this mess?"

"Oh, no, sir. The bird didn't do this. I did. I mean, I thought I'd just remove the end and use the vacuum hose to clean the bottom of the cage. That way I wouldn't spill seeds on the carpet."

"And?" Max prompted, focusing his frustration on Jody. What he wanted to do was seal off the room and never use it again. All he could do was glower at the boy who was gamely trying to explain the situation.

"I'm sorry, sir. How was I to know that the suction was strong enough to yank the little bird up? There was a whoosh, and it was gone."

"Excuse me, Mr. Sorrenson," Kate finally said quietly. "But we have a bird to take care of now. We can discuss this later. Jody, we need warm towels and a hair dryer. Let's go to the laundry."

Kate brushed past Max into the hall. She was walking away from him.

The thought that she was leaving shocked Max

into action. Even with her face smeared a shade of mummy gray, she was beautiful.

"No. This way," Max interceded calmly. "My suite is closer. "There's a portable dryer, towels, and an empty cage."

"But . . ." Kate started to protest, took one look at Max's face, and swallowed her words. She'd considered their next meeting, dreaded it, anticipated it, fantasized about it. Now he'd returned at the worst possible time. The bird in her pocket was probably suffocating, and she wasn't doing much better. The bird had to come first. She could wait. Kate followed Max. Jody was one step behind.

Max held up his hand, bringing Jody to a stop. "You clean up this room. If there's one speck of dust anywhere, you'll be selling hot dogs at the Burger Doodle." Max took Kate by the arm and closed the door firmly behind them, leaving Jody to repair the damage.

The elevator door opened as soon as the button was pushed, and Kate realized after a moment that Max had programmed it to wait for him.

"Kate, I—"

"Max, I—"

"You first—"

"No, you."

Tension hung between them.

"Ah, hell." Max hit the button that brought the elevator to a lurching stop and leaned over. "I've thought about kissing you for the last few days, and I don't care if you do look like a bag lady, I'm not going to wait another minute."

"Wait—your suit. You'll get dirty."

"I always did like gray."

Kate couldn't help herself. He had such kissable

lips. She groaned silently and she felt as if her heart had lodged in her throat. Max had to hear it thudding. It was pounding so hard that guests could probably hear the sound vibrating down the elevator shaft like a drumbeat in a silent jungle. Closing her eyes, she let her mind whirl away as her thoughts lost definition, changing into pure sensation.

Max put one hand behind her head to steady her and took her chin in his fingertips, holding her for the longest time before he lowered his head and pressed his lips to hers. His tongue invaded her mouth and sensation rocked him like a sudden burst of heat from a blast furnace. His hands held her immobile beneath the onslaught of his kiss. For a moment she allowed herself to respond, giving herself over to him freely with passion before stepping away.

"Max, stop. Please. There's a bird that's practically comatose in my pocket. I think we'd better take care of business, hadn't we?"

"What is there about you, Kate, that makes me forget about my responsibilities? You have me tied in knots, and I've never been this way before. It's incredible."

Then the bird chirped and they both stared at each other in dismay. Kate pulled away and shook her head.

"We have to clean the bird and warm it. It's probably in shock. I have to wash it, and I know that that will drop its temperature even more. I did some plumbing work for a veterinarian."

"On-the-job training. I should have known," he said warmly. He touched the elevator button, and the machine began to rise.

As he opened the penthouse door, he was smiling. He couldn't seem to help himself. Even the shadowy imprint on the front of his white linen jacket didn't disturb him. He simply slid the jacket off and let it fall to the floor as they walked.

In a few minutes, Kate was sitting on the edge of the tub in Max's bathroom, cleaning the bird's eyes and beak with a damp cloth. "I need warm towels, Max, and the hair dryer."

"Towels coming up. The dryer is on the counter behind you." Max picked up two towels and headed for the kitchen. Kate heard the sound of the microwave and smiled. She wet a second cloth and completed the washing procedure. Once she was satisfied, she turned the hair dryer on low and began to fluff the bird's feathers.

Max brought the warm towels and laid them on the tub beside Kate. "Why is it so still?"

"Shock does that to birds. Sometimes they die for no reason, other than fear." By the time she'd finished drying the bird, it had already begun to chirp more loudly. Kate took one of the warm towels and carefully wrapped the tiny creature.

Max watched Kate's gentle ministrations with awe. She must have been a good nurse for her mother—compassionate, tender. At the same time, she had to be tough as nails to take on a man's job. Some woman, this jack-of-all-trades who was prepared to be everything to everybody who needed her, as long as it wasn't on a permanent basis.

"Max, you said that you had a cage up here?"

"Oh, yes. In here, in the bedroom. Once I had a cockatoo. Dorothea thought I might be lonely and want someone to talk to."

"Did you?" Kate followed him.

"Maybe, but it wasn't a bird I needed."

Kate placed the bird in the ornate cage in the

corner and covered the cage with the second towel.
"What happened to it?"

"One day it just died. Probably from loneliness.
I should have talked to it. I missed you, Kate. I
missed talking to you. I missed kissing you. Kiss
me, Kate."

"Max, I can't. Not now, I'm on duty."

"You work for me, Kate. I'm taking you off duty.
You've been on call for two days. Relieving you of
duty for several hours is reasonable."

Kate studied Max. Reasonable, yes. Right? She
wasn't sure. But it was hard to think about right
and wrong when she looked at him. In fact, it was
almost impossible.

The man didn't simply wear clothes, he was the
body they'd been created for. He was everything
any woman could want, everything she could want.
It made no sense. He'd seen her at her worst.
Still, there he was, lips parted, eyes shooting darts
of fire through her, and she knew that she was
sunk.

"Kate? Please. Stay with me. I'll order something sent up, and . . ." He knew that he was
being unreasonable, he even understood her
insisting on doing Joe's job. But Max wasn't a
patient man. When he made a decision, he moved
swiftly. And somewhere between New York and
the hotel, he'd decided. He wanted Kate—at his
side, in his arms, and in his bed. Yet she was
standing there, holding him off, and he didn't
know how to get by the wall she'd erected between
them.

"You'll have something sent up? No, I think
not. I may not be able to stay out of your arms,
but I won't compromise myself by shirking my
job. I made a commitment to fill in for Joe, to do

Joe's work for two weeks. And that's what I'm going to do."

"So, I'll break another pipe. You can rewire the refrigerator. But I'm not letting you go."

"Well, I'm scheduled for a fifteen-minute coffee break. Do you have any coffee, Max?"

"Coffee? I'm dying from wanting to kiss you, and you want coffee?"

"I always have something sweet with my coffee. Maybe we could just skip the coffee altogether. Are you sure you know what you're doing here, bossman?" Her voice was low and hoarse.

"Sure? No, I'm not sure at all. This could be a very bad idea. I suspect it is. But I made up my mind when I left New York that I was going to reach out for life and live every minute of it, and I'm reaching."

Kate took the tab of the zipper that fastened her coveralls and gave it a jerk. She hadn't known she'd be so nervous about making love with Max again. But she was. On the island, it had been a fantasy. Being in the penthouse made her feel strange.

The zipper wouldn't budge. Raising her gaze, she shook her head wryly. "I'm stuck."

Her endearing little smile wiped away the tension, and Max felt his heart begin to sing.

"Let me help."

At that moment, Kate looked past Max and caught sight of herself in the mirrored wall of the foyer.

"Yuck!"

Max stiffened and withdrew the hand he'd extended. "What's wrong?"

"Oh, Max. I look as if I've been in the vacuum bag. You have weird taste in women." She pulled off her cap and ran her fingers through the dark tangles of her hair. "How on earth could you find me attractive?"

"Beats me. I've been out of control from the moment you tried to drown me that first night. Kiss me, Kate."

"I'll ruin your clothes if I get close to you."

"Hell, Kate." He lost all patience and jerked her to him. "I'll take 'em off." He ripped off his tie and shirt, stepped out of his shoes, unzipped his pants, and let them drop to the floor.

Shyly, Kate slid her arms up his chest and around his neck. She leaned back and let her eyes devour him. He was quite simply the most magnificent man she'd ever seen. And he was holding her against him, flexing his fingers across her lower back so tightly that she could hardly breathe. She stretched to reach his lips, feeling the distinct evidence of his desire pressing intimately against her midsection.

She parted her lips for his kiss, tasting, sampling, accepting what he was offering and returning it with undisguised passion.

The touch of his tongue kindled the ever-present flame smoldering inside her, turning her bones into hot wax. She moaned and swayed, allowing him to support her entirely. When his hand touched her breast, she shifted her position, arching herself into his palm.

"Kate, I've just introduced a new policy. Coffee breaks have been extended to thirty minutes."

"Good idea, Max."

The coveralls fell to her ankles.

Dimly, Kate heard the elevator door open.

"Hot damn!" Dorothea Jarrett slapped her knees

and clapped. "I don't have to ask where the fire is. Poor Kate's already been singed."

Kate leaned against the door of her room and cringed. She couldn't believe what had happened. It was bad enough that she'd come on to Max like some kind of sex kitten. She'd gone even further than that. She'd lost all control and practically attacked the man.

If Dorothea Jarrett hadn't opened the elevator door and discovered Max and her kissing passionately, they'd have been making love right there in the foyer in another minute. Her heart was still pounding, and her pulse was playing hopscotch.

Kate, unable to face the embarrassment of what had happened, had pulled up her coveralls, fled through the fire escape door, and descended all ten flights to the lobby on foot. Breathlessly, she'd passed a startled Helen Stevens in the lobby and had hurried down the walkway to her room.

Both bouquets of flowers from Max were still on Joe's dressing table, a reminder of the man from whom she'd just run.

She was tearing off her clothes when the phone rang. Her inclination to ignore it was short-lived. If she didn't answer it, he'd only be outside her door pounding to get in.

"Hello."

"Kate, I'm sorry. I know how embarrassed you must be. You must think I'm some kind of maniac. I lost control, and that's something I never do. I think we ought to talk."

"Talk? We don't seem to be able to talk unless we make love. And I don't know how to handle that. I never intended to let myself get involved with anybody, Max. I don't seem to be able to stay out of your arms now that we've . . ."

He groaned. "I know. We have to work it out. Will you have dinner with me? I promise that I won't try to force you into anything. Just dinner in the hotel restaurant, a neutral zone."

"Why?"

"To set some terms for our relationship." Max kept his voice light and unemotional.

"You mean to work this out like a business negotiation?"

"Dammit, Kate. Why do you keep doing this to me? How do I know what I mean? How do I talk to you? As a businessman or a lover? I've never been in love before. I never wanted to be. I don't know the rules."

"Love? Oh, no! You can't be falling in love with me, Max. I won't allow it. This—whatever this is—is temporary. Temporary, you understand. I'll finish up the job, and I'll be gone. If you want to have any kind of relationship with me, those are my terms."

"Fine. But I ought to warn you, I think Dorothea is going for her shotgun."

"Shotgun?"

"She has some kind of crazy idea that you've compromised her nephew's virtue," he said with all the seriousness of a deputy sheriff reading Kate her rights. "She says that she expects me to marry you."

"If this is an attempt at humor, I don't think it's very funny," Kate said, close to tears of pure frustration.

"You're right. It isn't funny. Oh, Kate, this is all my fault. I blew it." His voice was hoarse. "All I know is that I want you. Dirty, dust-covered, or soaking wet, you've gotten to me, lady. And I think we should take the time to find out what we have."

"Time? You forget, I'm only going to be here for a little over a week."

"You can stay longer. I'll find you another job. You can be my secretary."

"Max, I avoided the business courses in night school like the plague. I have no talent for business. If I tried to help you, you'd fire me in one day."

"Okay. We'll find something. I don't know what. Just give us a chance. Dorothea was right. I need to learn to have fun. If you won't have dinner with me tonight, will you go with me tomorrow? I promise I'll be on my best behavior. You won't have to fight me off more than once or twice."

"Tomorrow?"

"The Blessing of the Fleet, remember?"

Kate didn't know how to answer him. Did she want to go? Yes. Did she want to have to fight him off? No. She wanted to run right back up those stairs and finish what they'd started. Could she trust herself to spend an entire day with him?

Probably not, but that didn't matter. She wanted the day. She wanted to be with the man as long as they were away from the hotel. And she only had a short time left.

"Yes," she said softly. "I'll go with you, Max."

"Fine. I'll have the car out front at six o'clock."

"So early?"

"Yes, we're going to watch the sun rise, remember? Though I'd rather it be from my terrace, after you've spent the night in my arms."

Kate gasped. "This conversation is becoming very suggestive, bossman. Are you standing in front of the mirrors?"

"Why do you ask?"

"Because I am, and what I'm seeing is definitely X-rated. Good-bye, Max. I have some sooty finger-prints to wash off my body."

"You mean I left my brand on you?"

"You left your fingerprints on me, Max." *And you've put your brand on me in ways I never counted on*, she wanted to say. And she wasn't certain that there was enough water in the world to wash those marks away.

"I was never allowed to write on walls, but I like the idea of putting my brand on you. Getting to know you, Kate Weston, is one hell of an educa-tional experience."

"How's that?"

"Well, let's just say that I've been doing a little research into the world of movies and television. At this moment, I'd rather be Humphrey Bogart than either Cesar Romero or Lorenzo Lamas."

"Why is that?"

"I think his line was, 'Here's looking at you kid.' At least, that's what the book said. And if I were there, or you were here, that's what I'd be doing."

"Good-bye, Humphrey."

"Good-bye, Kate. I'll see you tomorrow."

As Kate replaced the receiver, it occurred to her that the word *see* had taken on an entirely differ-ent meaning, and that both she and Max had to open their eyes. Could they possibly have any kind of relationship?

Max wasn't falling in love with her. She was just different. She remembered what her mother had told her. Be careful. The first man you meet who's different can break your heart.

She and Max both had firsthand experience with the kind of pain that love brought. They'd both lost their mothers, and their lives had been shaped by love and the loss of it. No, it was better not to look on anything or anybody as permanent. Two weeks with pay and Max. That was all she'd let herself believe in.

"I don't know why Mr. Sorrenson called me, Ms. Stevens," Willie, the daytime maintenance man, said solemnly. "There weren't nothing wrong with that door. It didn't even stick."

"Don't worry about it, Willie," Helen said with a smile. "There wasn't anything wrong with the light bulb that buzzed on and off when you were at lunch either, but I changed it anyway."

"Is the man freaking out?" Willie's question was one of pure concern. "He ain't acting right. First he gives us thirty-minute coffee breaks and now he actually wants to talk—to me."

"Oh, I'm sure he'll be all right." Helen smothered a grin. "I think he just needs a good vacation. Mrs. Jarrett tells me that he's about to take a fishing trip."

When Kate reached the hotel lobby the next morning, her heart took a joyful leap at the sight of Max. Wearing sharply creased jeans and a soft blue knit shirt, he was breathtaking. He opened the door and pulled her close, right there in front of anyone who might be watching, silencing her greeting with a kiss.

"I didn't know what to wear," Kate said, pulling away. "I hope I look all right."

Max studied her for a moment. Her rich dark hair was caught at the sides with two combs, revealing her small square face. She'd left off her makeup this morning, and she looked fresh and innocent in her sailor blouse with the red and blue trim. She also wore bright red slacks and matching canvas shoes.

"You look perfect. I love a blouse with buttons in front."

Quickly, he escorted her to his car, closed the door, and moved around to the driver's side. Once inside, before starting the engine, he looked at her and said softly, "It was a very long night, Kate. Because of you I watched three old movies and made my own dinner. Did you sleep well?"

"Not a wink. I sat up all night making lists."

"You made lists? What kind?"

"A game plan, I guess you'd call it. I didn't want to make any mistakes."

"Did you bring it with you?"

"No, I decided that I don't do things logically. I never have, so why start. I'm off duty now, Max. Aren't you going to kiss me again?"

Kate read the answer in his eyes and leaned forward to meet his lips halfway. There was nothing halfway about the kiss he gave her, however, nor about her uninhibited response. When she pulled back, she felt his fingertips touch her shoulder possessively. She liked being joined to him, feeling a physical connection between their bodies. Kate let the cool early morning breeze caress her face. Life was good. This morning she felt right with the world.

"You look like the cat who swallowed the canary," Max said, as he started the engine.

"I feel wonderful. Speaking of canaries, how is the victim of the attack of the vacuum cleaner?"

"I returned him to his own cage. But I doubt

he'll ever be the same again. He seems to have fallen in love with the hair dryer."

"Where are we going?"

"First we stop at the doughnut shop," he said, and he promptly did, bringing back a familiar pink and white striped bag that he handed to Kate. "And then we turn down this road, where we should find just the right spot to watch the sun come up."

Max pulled the car in, backed it up, and positioned it so that they were perched on a hill facing east.

By the time he cut off the engine and reached for Kate's hand, the gray dawn sky was already changing. An orange ball seemed to float into the sky, and the world turned light. Kate had been holding her breath because of the sheer beauty before her. Now she released it in wonder and turned to look at Max. He was gazing at her with a hunger as powerful as the miracle of nature she'd just watched.

"What have you done to me, Kate? I've just spent days in meetings where I didn't hear half of the discussion. My appointment book is blank. I haven't even set up my weekly schedule. When I walk through the lobby, every woman I see is you. And you've got me mopping bathrooms, giving baths to birds, and watching old movies."

"I don't know," she said, sighing happily, "and I don't want to worry about it. All I want right now is this beautiful morning and breakfast with the man of my moment." What she wanted to do was sit and look at him, drink in the sight of him, believe that it was all real.

"That's a strange way to put it. I thought the phrase was the man of *the* moment."

"Maybe, but this is my moment, and for now, for today, you're the man I want to share it with. How about this breakfast you promised me?"

A sea gull called out shrilly, and Max jerked his gaze away, shaking his head. "In the bag. You're holding it. Ah, to hell with breakfast," he said gruffly, taking the bag and swinging it outside onto the roof of the car. "I don't want food. What I want is you, to kiss you and to touch you and to feel you against me for just a few minutes while we're still alone."

He did, and Kate opened her mouth and drank in the essence of him. And then they shifted to the back seat. She felt herself slip down, slide back against the door rest, the weight of his body pressing against her. He groaned and shifted his position, pushing the front seat forward into the car horn, which began to blare.

"Damn!" As Max struggled back across the seat, his knee knocked the gear into neutral, and the car began to roll backward slowly down the incline toward the water.

Kate sat up, watching Max wildly trying to untangle their legs and position his feet on the brake to bring the car to a stop. The horn continued to blow. He put the car in park, got out, and lifted up the hood.

The scene was too much. Kate began to laugh. When Max finally managed to jerk loose the wiring that controlled the insistent blare, he lifted his head, cracking the hood against the back of his neck.

"Shoot! If this isn't something straight out of a Steve Martin movie, I don't know what is." He began to laugh, too, and Kate found him even more endearing. By the time he'd gotten back inside the car, she had returned to the front seat. She leaned over to rub his head in exaggerated concern.

"Well, your few minutes were up, anyway."

"You go by your watch, and I'll go by mine. I feel injured." He assumed a sad pose.

"Ah, and I told you I'd teach you to have fun. Want me to kiss it and make it well?"

"Your kisses were what started all this," he said with mock anger. "Can't you be passionate without us ending up in the Gulf? What is it about you and water?"

"When a mere mortal dares to make love to a sea nymph, he gets in trouble."

"We'll settle this later," Max promised as he planted a whisper of a kiss on her lips. "I promise. Sea nymph or not, I'm too old to start making out in the back seat of a car. I have someplace more comfortable in mind when this mortal makes love to this sea nymph."

"Now?" Kate inquired with put-on innocence, "on an empty stomach?"

"No, later. Now we have a date with a preacher, and as our breakfast is floating away with the tide, we'll have to stop down the beach and eat real food."

"A preacher?"

"The Blessing of the Fleet, remember?"

"Oh, phooey. I thought Dorothea had made good her threat."

"You've never been married, have you, Kate?"

"No. You?"

"No. I never thought that I'd consider marriage. Ever."

Kate felt her heart make a funny little quiver. Did he mean that he was thinking about marriage now?

The fluttery feeling that had come over her when he'd mentioned marriage was still with her when Max pulled into the parking lot of a famous pancake house. Kate never even tasted the strawberry pancakes she ordered. Soon they were leaving, and it seemed as if they'd just arrived. At least that's what Kate thought, until she looked at her watch and saw that they'd been there for nearly two hours.

Kate smiled. Max whistled. And the day seemed full of promise.

Seven

"There was a church service earlier," Max explained as they made their way down the pier thronged with boisterous onlookers. "Now the boat captains, along with their families and crews, go to their boats and pass by the dock one at a time to receive the blessing."

The serious young minister stood at the end of the pier. Suddenly his black robe was caught by the breeze, and it ballooned up like great bat wings, revealing dark socks and red and black jogging shoes. Kate giggled out loud.

"Your minister either has a heavy schedule, or he believes in being prepared."

"What do you mean?" Max questioned.

"Look at his feet."

Max watched, waiting until the next gust of wind revealed the source of Kate's amusement.

"If you'd been here last year, you'd appreciate that even more. Most of the time our weather is clear and hot. But last year a sudden rainstorm blew up, and just as Reverend Knight blessed the last boat, the wind got under his robe and lifted him out into the water like a flying squirrel with no place to land."

"What he needed was flippers."

"You're right about that. His swimming was no better than his flying, and he nearly drowned. Eventually they hauled him up in Carlos's fishing net. I think there is still a picture on the church bulletin board proclaiming Reverend Knight as the prize catch of the year."

Kate examined Reverend Knight more closely. The robe was suspiciously bulky. She decided that the deck shoes weren't the only precaution the Reverend had taken. He was obviously wearing a life jacket under that robe.

The crowd began to swell, and Kate felt Max's arm move protectively around her, pulling her close. The gaily decorated boats began to move, one by one, past the end of the dock. The minister raised his hand and said the special blessing.

"Kate?" Max whispered in her left ear, innocently nibbling little teasing bites along her neck. "Let's get away from this crowd. I want to take you on board one of the boats. I've arranged for Carlos Herrera to pick us up a bit further down."

They moved out of the crowd and down the dock to where a shorter pier reached out into the bay. In a few minutes a small, brightly painted boat strung with colored flags chugged up to where they were waiting.

"Kate. I'm glad you're going out with us," Helen Stevens called from on board. "Hello, Mr. Sorrenson." Her voice dropped a bit, as though she were not quite sure how to respond to her employer.

"Nice to see you, Helen. I didn't know you'd be

here," Max answered easily as he helped Kate step down into the gently rocking boat. "This is Carlos, the captain of this floating birthday cake. Carlos used to work for me."

"What Mr. Sorrenson means is that this boat used to belong to him. It's partly mine now."

"Yeah, Carlos offered me a deal I couldn't turn down. We're partners now. He's going to let us share a traditional Feast Day celebration. All you need is candles on this thing, Carlos."

"Glad you could come, sir," Carlos said, "and Helen's with me. I hope you don't mind."

"Today I don't mind anything, Carlos. Today is a grand day for . . . having friends."

Helen looked curiously at her employer and then back at Carlos. "You're going to love this, Kate," she said proudly. "All the boats move out into the bay and drop anchor side by side. Then each of us spreads out our picnic, so to speak, and we all move from boat to boat and share our feasts."

"And whatever kind of alcoholic brew these pirates have concocted," Max added. "And don't call me 'sir.' Today I'm Max."

There was no mistaking Carlos's startled look. But Helen's friendliness made up for the awkwardness, and soon they were all chatting freely.

There were three other crew members on board, along with wives and sweethearts. In jeans and deck shoes, Max fit right in with the others, and Kate felt comfortable too.

Max stood, his arm draped lazily but possessively around Kate's waist. Occasionally he would whisper in Kate's ear. The crew quickly accepted Kate as his girl, and she began to accept it too. His private comments and constant touching made her glow.

"We make our way to the middle of the lagoon," Max explained, "where the other boats are already circled like a wagon train ready to stave off an Indian attack. Then comes the food, drink, fun, and sex."

"Sex?" Kate gasped.

"Oh, that's later. A private party, just me and you."

He was putting her on notice, and her body quivered.

"Hold on, darling, don't let your eagerness show."

"The boat moved," she insisted, moving out of Max's reach.

"Yeah," he agreed with a smile. "I felt it too."

Helen and the other women quickly began to spread out red and white checked cloths and open their baskets. There were chilled bottles of wine, homemade bread, chunks of thick sliced meats, even a broiled stuffed chicken that looked suspiciously like the one she'd seen in the hotel kitchen earlier. She was told that the other boats would have boiled shrimp and other kinds of fish, chowders, stews, and tasty pastries.

"Max." Carlos motioned to a boat approaching their circle. It was a smaller boat, neat and clean, but not nearly as well kept. "I think there will be trouble here, my friend. The skipper is one of the newcomers."

"No," Max said quietly, and motioned for the boat captain to pull up alongside Carlos's boat. The others were silent and all eyes were turned to the newcomer. When the vessels were side by side, Max smiled and leapt lightly across the short expanse of water between them.

"Will you share our food?" the thin man asked with a hesitant smile.

"He's from Louisiana, where an oil spill killed off all the fish," Helen whispered. "He came here three months ago, and since then the other fishermen have been out of their minds with worry that he's only the first."

"Does Max know him?"

"Probably not," Helen whispered. "But at least Max has the reputation of being willing to examine all sides of an issue. This boat isn't really much in the way of competition; it's the possibility of more competition that Carlos and the others are afraid of."

Kate vaguely remembered watching something on television about the oil spill and the subsequent pollution that had killed the fish in the area. Local fishermen had been forced to move or find other means of earning a living. Kate couldn't help but feel a little sorry for the stoop-shouldered little man and his wife who were timidly holding out pots of food.

Kate considered the rocking boats for a moment, then caught the side of the rail and cautiously stepped across to stand beside Max. When she smiled and looked into the pot with what she hoped was an expression of delight, she heard Max's satisfied sigh.

In a few minutes, Helen followed Kate's lead and came over to bring fried chicken to the strangers and sample the creole dish they'd offered. Soon one of the other boats pulled alongside and two burly looking, weather-beaten old men came aboard, tasted the food, left a bottle of wine, and moved on to the next boat.

Finally the newcomers shook Max's hand and waved to Kate and Helen as they moved back to Carlos' boat.

"Thank you, Kate," Max said simply, the pride in his voice giving way to something deeper. He moved nearer and put his arm around her, pulling her close once more.

"I feel sorry for those people. Pollution hurts all of us, but the little guy is often crushed. The larger fleets have more power. They can sell for higher prices, and because they buy more, they can get their supplies for less too. The others have to fish twice as much to make a living. Carlos is right. Trouble is brewing," Max said.

"Too bad they can't all join together," Kate commented, thinking how kind Max really was. "I mean, if they were all equal, the owners of the small boats wouldn't have to fish so much. They could set some kind of rules or something."

The sun was dropping behind a bank of purple clouds just above the edge of the ocean, and the wind had begun to blow. Kate shivered, not entirely as a result of the cool night air, and moved deeper into the circle of Max's arms.

From the other boats, the sound of guitars and concertinas began and the fishermen started to sing. Max and Kate sat on the deck listening in the darkness.

It was very late when they made their way back to the dock.

"Thank you, Max," Kate whispered, "for a lovely day."

"I haven't forgotten my promise," he said as he put his arm around her, and they walked slowly to the parking area.

"Oh, and what was that?"

"Breakfast and a sunrise, especially ordered, privately for two."

"Max, you've already fulfilled both parts. The

sunrise was spectacular and the breakfast was too."

They reached the car, and Max reluctantly started the engine. Kate leaned her head against the seat and closed her eyes. She'd never had such a day. She hadn't believed it was possible. At the close, she didn't want to think of anything that might spoil it. The light fragrance of flowers mingled with the faint woodsy odor of Max's cologne, and Kate felt very good.

They drove for some time in comfortable silence before Max spoke. "Today was nice, Kate. You're easy to be with—no pretense, nothing phony. You didn't look down on the fishermen. I think I like that very much."

Kate didn't answer. She took a deep breath and turned toward him, feeling a sharp pain cut into her. He was the most beautiful man she'd ever seen, and she wanted so much to reach out and touch him. She wanted to tell him that she felt good with him. But she knew that this couldn't be real, not the forever kind of real.

"Oh, Max, I'm not so special. You don't really know anything about me. You're seeing me through . . . special eyes."

"Oh? You have six children, a Great Aunt Bertha who's a bookie, and a great dane named Spot who hates men? No matter."

"No, none of those. I'm a blue-collar worker, Max. That's why I fit in with those people. They're like me. You were one of them today. But back at the hotel, in everyday life, you live in the penthouse. Don't make either of us something we're not. Let's just enjoy what we have for now. No promises, Okay?"

"Oh, I intend to do that, Kate. I'll decide what

kind of woman I need." He turned the car into the hotel parking lot and killed the engine, then reached out and took her chin in his hand.

"You're really something," he murmured softly. "And you don't even know it. What kind of men were there in that town back in Kentucky?"

"Pretty ordinary. As far as I know, we've only had two claims to fame."

"You and who else?"

"Not me—Dwight Yoakam and Joey Huffman. Dwight Yoakam just made a hit record."

Max raised one eyebrow. "Really?"

"And Joey, he's the keyboard man with a new rock group called Witness. They just got started. But they're going to be big."

Max raised the other eyebrow.

"He lived down the street from me. His mother was my mother's best friend."

"Lucky Joey. Kiss me, Kate."

"Why?"

"You're a nice person, Kate Weston, and you kiss nicely, too. Now, come with me."

He kissed her lips once more before he reluctantly released her, removed the keys from the ignition, and opened his door.

"Where are we going?"

"We're going up to the penthouse to work on my reference library."

"Not tonight, Max. I'm on call. Remember, I'm a working girl?" Kate gathered up her bag.

"So, be on call from the penthouse. You have your beeper."

"When I'm with you, Max, I don't think I'd hear any other bells ring. Besides," she said with a smile, "it would be very hard to leave you."

"But, Kate, I want you to stay with me, have

breakfast with me on my terrace. I want to watch you wake up, see if you squeeze the toothpaste in the middle. Is there anything wrong with that?" He grabbed her shoulder roughly and leaned her back against the car, pressing the full length of his legs and lower body against her.

His words caught her by surprise. And yet in a crazy way she recognized that he was right. "Max, this isn't going to make much sense, but it's the penthouse."

"The penthouse is where I live. Would you rather I lived on a fishing boat?"

"It's not really the place, Max, it's the commitment. Making love with you is too much like being in love. Making love in your penthouse, your home, might feel too comfortable. I don't know if I could move on afterward. Away from the penthouse, I still feel free. Now I have to get inside. The night manager might need me."

"By all means, Kate. I wouldn't want to come between you and an adventure. Heaven forbid that the plumbing, or the electricity, or an escaping bird would have to wait an hour for your services."

He got out of the car and walked around to open the passenger door. He didn't know what he was saying. Of course he wanted the guests cared for. The hotel was his responsibility. And he never wanted Kate to give up her spirit of adventure. He just wanted to *be* that adventure.

She hadn't intended to hurt Max. She hadn't wanted to think about tomorrow. Now they were back at the hotel. The clock had struck twelve, and she was a maintenance worker again.

"All right, Kate." Max's voice was low and strained. "But I don't intend to let this end here. You go on inside and keep the hotel safe from disaster. I have a business appointment away from the hotel tomorrow. While I'm gone, you think about us, Kate. You think about relationships and commitments. Because I know what I want. I want you."

Kate started to reach out to him, caught herself, and let her hand drop to her side. "You can't want me. Believe me, Max, it wouldn't work. I won't let you do this."

Kate whirled and ran across the parking area and into the garden. She reached her room, flung open the door, slammed it closed, and leaned back against it, breathing raggedly. For a long time all she heard was the sound of her breathing. Then she felt that curious sensation that always announced Max's presence to her, even when she couldn't see him.

"All right, Kate," he said from beyond the door. "But I want to thank you for the nicest day of my life. You don't think you that fit into my world, but I'm going to prove that you're wrong. Be ready tomorrow night. We're going to a Hotel Association business dinner. I'll pick you up at eight."

"Why?"

"I want you to meet the people in my world. You'll see that they aren't so very different from you and me. Kate?" His voice dropped to a whisper. "Will you open the door for a second? I won't try to come in. I just want to kiss you goodnight. Please?"

Kate opened the door.

His kiss wasn't demanding. It was sweet and gentle, and before he was finished, Kate knew that she'd go with him—anywhere.

"Sleep well, darling, until tomorrow night."

Kate watched him walk down the sidewalk, stop

by the pool, and give her a sweet smile. She wanted to go with him. It was all she could do to stay in the doorway and watch him leave. Finally she loosened her hold on the frame, blew him a kiss, and fled into her room before she gave in to her feelings and ran back into his arms.

If Kate closed her eyes after Max left, she wasn't aware of it. Eventually in desperation she pulled on a pair of shapeless pants and a baggy shirt and walked down to a secluded part of the beach.

The sea was rough and angry, hurling frothy waves onto the shore in jerky slaps that broke the night silence, then retreated begrudgingly, leaving deep slashes in the sand. Gone was gentle crystal blue-green water, and Kate understood the uneasy turbulence that churned the sea. She felt drained beyond anything she'd ever imagined. The cottony grayness wrapped around her like a cocoon, and she felt smothered by the heavy air.

Finally, chilled and weary, she drew herself up and moved back down the beach. From the garden she saw Max, dressed in a soft blue suit, stop and speak to Ricardo, the night manager. Ricardo looked pleased.

Kate decided that Ricardo was seeing a new side of his employer, an employer who was recognizing the individual faces of his staff. If you'd asked Max a week ago what Ricardo looked like, or who the gardener was, he wouldn't have known. Max was changing. Could she? Could a woman who had grease on her nose more often than cold cream ever really fit in to whatever relationship Max envisioned? Could what she was feeling be love?

Kate shook her head and wished she had the magical powers of the gods. Life had been hard while her mother had been ill, but it had been easier too. She'd done what she had to do. Her life had been orderly, different from Max's, but regimented just the same.

Afterward, she'd fled from that order, determined never to be responsible for anyone but herself again. Now her carefree life was being threatened. She was changing too. And it frightened her because she didn't know who she was becoming, and Max didn't understand who she had been.

"He's never taken anyone to the festival before. As far as I know, he's never even been on the boats," Helen Stevens observed later as she and Kate shared a late lunch.

"Really? I don't understand. I mean, why be interested in me? He could have his pick of any woman in the state of Florida." Kate toyed with her food.

"Sure, and he's paraded a few of them through here at night and sent them home by the hotel courtesy car afterward. But this is different. He's different. Yesterday he treated Carlos and me as friends not just employees. And this morning he asked Ricardo to set up one-on-one interviews with everyone on the staff. He wants to get to know them. That's a real change."

"I don't know what to say. That's very nice," Kate agreed, still remembering how much she'd liked being Max's woman. It felt right when she was with him. Why then did she have such doubts when they'd gotten back to the hotel? Was it the hotel that intimidated her? No—it was what the hotel represented that held her back.

"It was more than nice, Kate. Max has always been fair, but sometimes it's been hard to explain staff problems to a man in his position."

"We're both changing," Kate admitted. "And the change is hard to deal with."

"By the way, Mrs. Jarrett's companion, the lovely Lucy Pierce, is finally back. You'd better stay away from her. She has her eye on Max, and she wouldn't think twice about running over you in the process."

"Lucy Pierce? Where has she been, anyway?"

"If you ask me, knowing Lucy, I'd say she's been with a man. She took off rather suddenly. Said it was family business. Business? Hah! I'd like to tell you more, but I'm due back at the desk. Just watch out for Lucy."

Later, in the laundry room, Kate took a telephone call from Mrs. Jarrett.

"Kate, you need to keep that fishing line tight. Max is beginning to weaken, and it's time to start reeling him in."

"Mrs. Jarrett, I wish you wouldn't talk like that. By the way, I heard that your companion is back."

"Only for the moment," Dorothea said guardedly. "How are you?"

"Not very well, I'm afraid. Every time I'm with Max, everything gets more confused. I just seem to make everything worse."

"Fiddle-faddle, if this is worse, I can't wait for total disaster," Mrs. Jarrett said with a chuckle. "I'm so pleased. You've done so well with what you've had to work with that I've sent you some more."

"More what?"

"You'll see. Are you ready for tonight?"

"Tonight? We're going to some Association party. I have to go so that he can prove to me that I fit into his life. Why on earth would he want me there?"

"I think if he had his way, you'd be everywhere with him. I was up to the penthouse earlier, and he has his Old Spice, his Frank Sinatra records, and a sign blinking DO NOT DISTURB in neon lights on the elevator door."

"Yes, well," Kate said nervously, "I'm afraid he does expect me to stay the night."

"Hot damn! I knew it."

Kate didn't know how to respond.

"Don't go shy on me, girl. Are you?"

"Mrs. Jarrett, you're incorrigible." Kate ended the conversation when she heard the sound of water sputtering in one of the washing machines behind her. "Have to go, more plumbing work to do."

She simply wouldn't go, she told herself the whole time she was dressing. She'd explain that the idea was ludicrous. She'd just wait until he returned and meet him for a late dinner in the hotel dining room. They'd be able to talk there. Then later, if it seemed like the thing to do, she'd go with him to his suite. Maybe she'd stay the night.

Kate was almost ready when the phone rang.

"Kate, this is Ricardo. I thought I'd tell you that a delivery boy just took a package to the penthouse for you."

"A package for me? What is it?"

Ricardo laughed. "I don't think I'm going to say. You wouldn't believe me if I did. One thing I will say is that my job has certainly become more interesting since you came to work here. I want to thank you for putting in a good word for me with the boss. I definitely deserve the raise."

If she'd been nervous before, Kate was in a state of full panic now. She surveyed herself in the mirror. She didn't have the smoldering exotic look she'd achieved the night of the first party. The dark green dress she wore was simple and un-adorned. It brought out the green flecks in her eyes. She'd created a simple hairstyle by drawing her hair straight back into a bun and securing it with a bronze Spanish comb that had been a gift from Helen.

With a light touch of eye shadow, a heavier than usual application of mascara, a simple gold bracelet, and strappy shoes, she was ready.

All the way to the penthouse, Kate tried not to think about what she was doing, about what her going there implied, or what she expected to happen. Her mouth had gone dry, and she moist-ened her lips nervously. As she stepped off the elevator she walked straight into a large bushel basket filled with bright yellow lemons.

Lemons? Mrs. Jarrett popped immediately into Kate's mind. *I like a woman who uses lemons to make lemonade.* Mrs. Jarrett had said that the first night. Kate wondered what Max thought of his aunt's gift.

The weakness is Kate's knees intensified when she read the message on the card that was ad-dressed to her.

If your line breaks, squeeze.
                                        Dorothea

The door was open, and Kate smiled as she walked through the apartment. From somewhere in the back, she could hear the sound of piano music. She couldn't be certain but she thought she recognized the lovely voice of Rossano Brazzi singing "Some Enchanted Evening." Max was showing his new interest in movies, no doubt.

The terrace door was ajar, bringing the clean smell of the sea inside. Kate wandered outside into the still-light evening and looked out over the Gulf. There was a tranquil, unending beauty in the view. The sea seemed to reach out to some deeply hidden part of her, and she didn't know whether or not she'd ever want to live away from it now.

She'd left a life of routine and schedules after her mother had died, a life in which the only place she could let go was in her how-to classes.

Organized was what she'd had to be then. She hadn't had a choice with only so much time and money and so many demands on her. For the last two years, she'd moved from one place to another, never allowing herself to stand still. The whole world had beckoned to her, and she intended to see every inch of it. Work three months and move on—that was her philosophy.

One adventure after another, that's what she wanted. And Max was an adventure. That's all she'd allow him to be. Her mother had fallen in love with her adventurer. Kate would never allow herself to do the same.

She'd stop fighting him and enjoy whatever came. Moving on might be hard, but Max would be worth it. When had her life ever been easy, anyway? Kate closed her eyes and let the enchantment of the melody envelop her as she swayed to the rhythm of the music.

She whirled around, holding a phantom lover as the magic of the moment swept her away. When long, slim fingers clasped her outstretched hand, she moved willingly into her mystery lover's embrace, arching her body and lifting her other arm behind his neck. The imaginary dancer changed into a real-life man who paused for a moment, rocking back and forth in time with the music, before sliding one leg between hers and spinning her wildly around the patio. Coming at last to a breathless stop, she opened her eyes, reluctant to break the spell.

"Hello, darling. I've waited all day for this." Smoky eyes gazed at her hungrily before possessive lips captured her mouth with such passion that she moaned.

"Max," Kate finally whispered, gulping in a breath of air, "you're overwhelming. I don't know whether I'm coming or going. You're making me crazy." She unwound herself with weak-kneed uncertainty and moved to the balcony rail.

"You're coming to me, exactly where you should be, Kate," Max whispered, standing directly behind her. He reached out and circled her body, folding his arms beneath her breasts. She could feel the steady thud of his heart against her back and his breath against her hair.

"We have to talk, Max. I've made up my mind not to fight you anymore. I do want you. I don't know how this will work out, but if you trust me to fit in, I'll trust you to be right."

"Trust. That's an odd word to choose, Kate. I've never trusted a woman before. But I'm opening myself up to you, unequivocally. Be gentle, darling. I'm fragile." He nuzzled her ear. "Want to tell me why I have a basket of lemons in my entrance hall? I thought nectarines were the fruit of the gods."

Hands that had been content to hold now cupped her breasts, which peaked in immediate response. Max murmured in her hair and pressed his body against her, and Kate knew that she was lost.

"Nectarines? Only on Mount Olympus," she said with a moan and pressed her body wickedly against the man holding her.

Max gasped and continued to caress her breasts while his lips drew little circles on her shoulder and the back of her neck. Finally he drew back and said in a ragged voice, "As much as I want you, we have to leave now. We're expected at Red Garden's party in half an hour, and I have to be there."

His hands slid reluctantly from her throbbing breasts, and Kate took a deep breath before turning to face Max. She wanted to say something to let him know how she felt, but she couldn't. Not yet sure enough of her feelings, she walked away and he followed, not talking, not touching.

Max paused at the elevator, lifted Kate's hand, and lightly kissed her fingertips. "I dare not touch you again, Kate, though I want to kiss every part of you. I just want you to know that later, when we return, we have some serious decisions to make. And this time we aren't parting in the courtyard."

"Yes." Kate's voice had tightened so that a simple yes was all she could manage. The sound of the elevator door opening broke the intense silence. Max moved inside and turned to her expectantly. Kate reached down and picked up one lemon from the basket. She dropped it in her purse and stepped into the elevator and Max's waiting arms.

"Where are we going?" she managed to ask.

"We're going to meet the man who's buying the Showboat. The Showboat is the first piece of property that the Association has lost to an outsider."

Kate kept silent, waiting for him to continue. She knew he was disturbed about the sale. It would be like Max to assume full responsibility for the loss. She already knew how he feared for the purity of the strip.

"The buyer seemed to know exactly how we operate and how far we were able to go. Of course, the committee knew that we'd lose one sooner or later, but this man paid just enough more than we could afford to bid. There's something wrong about the timing and how he worked it all out."

"Maybe he's just a good businessman," Kate commented.

"Maybe, but the entire deal has been much too smooth for that. Still, the papers aren't actually final yet. The mortgage holder has to agree. But that's purely a formality. Red already has his check, pending approval by the lender. I guess that I feel as though some piece of the puzzle is missing, and I'm afraid that the failure might be my fault."

"You mean because of me?"

"You? Certainly not. Why would you think that?"

"You said you couldn't concentrate because you were . . ." her voice trailed off.

"Believe me, Kate, you had nothing to do with this. The man was just better prepared than we'd expected."

The Showboat loomed up before them like a Mississippi River boat, all brick red, gold, and lacy white. It was breathtaking. Kate couldn't hold back a gasp.

"It's something to see, isn't it? That's another thing that bothers me. Everybody knows that Red has no taste. Who would buy something that looks like a million-dollar brothel?" Max stopped the car and handed over the keys to the attendant.

"Well, it is very different," Kate agreed. The glass walls and rich velvet decor made her uneasy some-how, and she patted the lemon in her bag com-fortingly as they walked through the lobby and took the elevator to the penthouse suite.

"We were just about to give up on you, Max." A bald, portly man with a huge unlit cigar said as he came toward them. "The others are in the library."

"I was unavoidably detained," Max answered with a serious face and a side wink for Kate. "Kate, this is Red Garden. Red, Kate."

Red nodded to Kate and continued to move toward an open doorway in the back of the room. "I'd like you to meet the new hotel owner, Max, and then stick around later for dinner."

Red stopped at the door, looked at Kate, and back at the party guests clustered around the bar. "Perhaps you'd like me to introduce your lady to some of the others while you go on in."

"That isn't necessary," Kate said. "I see Mat-thew Blue heading this way. I'll talk with him until you're free."

Max released Kate reluctantly, touching his lips to her cheek gently. "This won't take too long, darling."

Matthew's bushy hair was more unruly than the first time Kate had seen him. She was glad to see his friendly face, and his smile widened appreciably when Kate met him halfway.

"Matthew, I'm so glad you're here."

Behind Matthew, Kate saw a tall, striking woman bearing down on them with a directness that was definitely not indicative of cocktail party circulating. Smooth, fawn-color hair cascaded down a body elegantly encased in a bronze gown.

"So, you're Kate. I'm Lucy Pierce," the woman said with a half-knowing smirk. "You're my replacement in the room at the top, I've been told. Fast work. But then, Max has always made it a point to look after his aunt's protégées."

"Oh, you're Lucy. I'm so glad to meet you," Kate said innocently. Lucy's welcome was as genuine as a thirty-dollar bill, and they both knew it. "Did you come with Mrs. Jarrett?"

"Why, no. Actually, I'm turning in my resignation. I've accepted another job, more prestige, more money. A girl has to look after her future. You certainly know about that," Lucy said sharply, quickly excusing herself when someone called from across the room.

Matt gave Kate's elbow a squeeze. "Don't let her get to you, Kate. Lucy Pierce is just blowing air bubbles. Max may have played around with her, but she's not even in the running."

"I know, Matthew," Kate assured the dear man. And she did. Lucy was obviously accustomed to receiving the attention of every man around, and Kate could understand why.

"What will you have to drink, Kate?" Matthew and Kate walked across a gold and black Oriental rug and stood near the piano where a handsome young man with a faraway look in his eyes played blues tunes.

"Just fruit juice, thanks," Kate said, glad to be somewhat isolated from the animated discussions taking place behind them. She knew that she was being observed discreetly, and the knowledge was disquieting.

As Matthew went to the bar, Kate looked at the guests. They were laughing, talking. Shades of J.R. and *Dallas*, she thought. The room was too bright and gay. Kate suddenly felt uncomfortable. Learning to fit in with Max's friends might be more nerve-racking than she'd imagined. She glanced around and quietly slipped through the sliding glass doors and out onto the terrace. She'd be more comfortable facing them with Max at her side.

Standing in the darkness, she looked at the ground below. The hotel was built on a piece of land that jutted out into the Gulf. The riverboat design of the building set it apart from it's neighbors.

Kate heard the terrace door opening behind her. "I'll step out here for a smoke while you talk about it, gentlemen," a masculine voice said, "but it won't change anything. I've outbid you, and Red has my check."

There was a sound of footsteps on the terracotta tile floor. A man moved through the shadows toward the corner where Kate was standing. He paused in a patch of light, pulled a silver cigarette case from his pocket, and snapped it open.

The scene was straight out of a Cary Grant movie. She watched, spellbound, as he touched a thin silver flame from an ebony lighter to the cigarette. A lazy puff of smoke floated across the air.

"Hello." The man moved toward her, replacing

the cigarette case. "Fellow refugee from the lion's den?"

"I suppose. It's a bit loud in there." Kate turned back to gaze at the sea.

"You prefer the solitude of the night? So do I." He walked up beside her.

She didn't answer.

"Are you one of Red Garden's friends, or one of the Hotel Association ladies?"

"Neither. I'm here with . . . someone." Kate didn't know why it was so hard for her to say Max's name.

"Too bad," the stranger commented with just the right amount of despair in his voice. "I thought you might like to join me later, for a drink."

"Thank you, but I think I'd better look for my friend."

"Please don't go on my account. After all, I'm the intruder. I promise I won't annoy you any more."

Behind them, inside the room, the piano player started to play a slow romantic tune.

"Quite a place, isn't this?" The stranger turned his back to the Gulf, resting his elbows on the rail as he looked into the room. "Like something out of the Gay 'Nineties, complete with the madam."

Madam? Kate followed his line of sight to Lucy Pierce glancing around with a look of irritation on her face. When she appeared to be heading in their direction, the stranger took Kate's shoulder and pulled her back into the shadows. "I'm sorry. I'm not trying to kidnap you. But that woman is someone we're both better off avoiding."

At that moment, Kate saw Max appear at Lucy's side. Lucy was motioning toward the balcony, and anger flashed across Max's face.

The sliding doors flew open, and Max crossed the terrace in four steps, jerking Kate away from the startled man at her side.

"Kate, how could you bring the very thing I've fought hardest against right into my own hotel? Dorothea was right. You've been working for *Maverick* magazine all along."

"That's absurd. I don't know anything about *Maverick* magazine? I don't understand. What's wrong?"

"What's wrong is that your editor, J.M. Houston, is the mysterious buyer, Kate. And I find you standing out here in the dark in his arms. You must be very happy."

J.M. Houston? Kate looked from Max to the dark stranger she'd been talking to. J.M. Houston?

This was *Vertigo*. She was Kim Novak and Alfred Hitchcock was directing her fall through space into a black void of nothingness.

Eight

"Max, no . . ." Kate whispered.

"I trusted you, Kate. I left myself wide open. I'll have to hand it to you, lady, you're brilliant, a professional from the word go. You had me fooled, and that doesn't happen very often."

Kate couldn't believe what was happening. Max was livid. Not only was he stern and unforgiving, but she could feel the heat of his anger in the fingers holding her arm in an iron grip.

"Just a minute, Max, aren't you being unreasonable?" Matthew Blue had moved to the edge of the circle. "I, for one, don't believe a word of it. Let's hear what Kate has to say."

"I didn't believe it either," Max said, desperation in his voice. "I told the committee that they were wrong. Kate couldn't work for him. Making Kate a writer for *Maverick* magazine was just one of Dorothea's little jokes."

Max saw the stricken look on Kate's face. Confusion gave way to hurt, then total disbelief. She jerked her arm from his grasp.

"Max," she said softly, "I don't even know J.M. Houston, and I haven't the slightest idea what you're talking about."

"Don't know him? Then how do you explain my finding you here with him at the very moment we're trying desperately to save the future of the Carnival Strip?"

"You're J.M. Houston of *Maverick* magazine?" Kate asked the man next to her. He nodded. "Then tell him the truth, Mr. Houston," Kate whispered raggedly. "Tell him that I had nothing to do with this."

"I did," he answered. "He didn't believe me either."

Kate felt the floor tilt. She wanted to disappear.

"Isn't it obvious, Max?" Lucy Pierce trilled. "J.M. sent her here to keep him informed while he made the arrangements. You fell for her, didn't you, Max? She probably spent a lot of time in your suite. It would have been easy for her to wait until you were gone, get the necessary figures, and pass them on to her boss."

Kate could tell that Lucy's words were hitting home. She'd had a key. Max knew that she had access to his office. And he believed that Mr. Houston had inside information. He thought she was guilty. Nothing she could say was going to change his mind.

"That's how he knew exactly how much to bid," someone volunteered from the crowd. "He had a mole. Isn't that right, Mr. Houston?"

The stranger blinked his eyes lazily and smiled. "Surely you gentlemen don't think I'd do anything illegal, do you? And I'd never reveal my sources. Let's just say that I do find this lovely lady very appealing."

"Kate," Max continued, "Kate, J.M. Houston, and the Showboat. Later, when he's been able to grease enough palms to swing votes in his direction, we'll have gambling on the Strip. All perfectly legal, thanks to his inside source. Thanks to you, Kate."

Matthew Blue caught Kate as her legs began to buckle, half supporting her as she tried to speak. "I swear, Max, I've never seen this man before in my life. I don't work for him, and I never have."

"She's right," Matthew snapped. "Kate working for *Maverick* magazine was just something your aunt cooked up. Tell him the truth, Houston. It can't matter to you now."

"Oh, I think having Kate work for *Maverick* magazine is a fine idea," J.M. agreed in amusement. "I've already made her an offer, which she turned down. Maybe now she'll reconsider."

But Max wasn't listening. He simply stared at Kate as though he'd never seen her before. "And I fell in love with you, Kate. For the first time in my life I was in love." He turned away.

"Max, wait. You're a smart businessman," Matthew called out, as he turned Kate toward the elevator, "but this time you're way off base."

Kate straightened her shoulders and allowed Matthew to propel her through the crowd to the elevator. She couldn't believe what had happened. Max thought that she'd betrayed him—Max, the man she loved. She hadn't even acknowledged to herself that she loved him until now. But it was true. Except there would be no happily ever after. Max couldn't care about her and still believe that she was involved in such a terrible scheme.

Somehow she got out of the suite and into Matthew's car. He headed away from the hotel, down the beach highway. Tears rolled down Kate's cheeks, and she sobbed in the silence. She didn't know when the car stopped or how long Matthew had been waiting before he said, "Max is wrong and I'm responsible. I should have spoken up sooner, but I wanted to find out how Houston managed to pull this off."

"I don't understand, Matthew. What could you have done? Max wasn't in the mood to listen to anybody."

"The sale was contingent on approval of the mortgage holder, Kate. That's me. I hold the mortgage on the Showboat, along with a half dozen other pieces of property along the strip. And I don't approve."

"You? But—" Kate's head was spinning. Max hadn't lost the hotel to an outsider, but she'd lost Max.

"I'll tell Max tomorrow," Matthew was saying, "when he's had time to think. I've seen him like this once before. He was just as hurt and angry then as he is now. I took him in and helped him get through it. I'll straighten this out too."

Kate didn't answer. Max didn't trust her and that couldn't be changed.

"Right now," Matthew went on softly, "I'm ready for something to eat besides those little cheese things they give you at those parties to soak up the booze. I never did like my liquor contaminated with junk."

"Where are we?" Kate looked around. They were parked in front of a cedar house made from thick beams. She could hear the sound of the sea in the distance. She allowed Matthew to help her from the car and down a flower-lined walk to an open, sparsely furnished room built out over the water.

"This is where I live," Matthew said proudly. "You wouldn't think an old sea pirate like me lived here, would you?" Kate stepped outside on the deck and breathed deeply. Matthew followed her.

"It's lovely, Matthew. It reminds me of a painting of yours I saw in a little beach art shop. There was a dark-eyed little boy watching the fishing fleet just at the edge of the horizon. You could almost see the tears in his eyes. He seemed very lonely."

"Yes. It was painted from the same spot where you're standing. If you look out at the sea, you can see just about where the fishing fleets disappear in the dawn."

It was dark now, and Kate had to envision the scene in her mind, but she knew how the boy must have felt. She wanted to go, too, to run away and disappear. But this time she wasn't looking for adventure.

"Kate, about Max's behavior tonight. I think it would help you to know why he was so angry."

"I don't care, Matthew."

"Maybe not, but listen to me anyway. It's all tied in with his mother and her drug addiction. He was just a kid when he found out. He'd built up some fantasy about her dying a tragic death. Dorothea couldn't tell him the truth about her sister. He heard the gossip."

"I know, she killed herself. Max told me."

Matthew looked surprised. "One summer Max came home from school. He'd never fit in very well there and that summer he went kind of wild. He got into drugs, but he realized he was in trouble and he came to me. I guess I was too blunt about telling him that drugs were the reason his mother committed suicide. But I wanted him to understand why he could never allow himself that weakness.

"After that, he seemed to understand why Dorothea wanted him to have a different kind of life. He set a quest for himself. He knew he could never stop people from taking drugs, but he'd keep drugs off the Strip. He's fighting a losing battle, but somebody's got to try."

"I understand, Matthew. Really I do. But how could he believe that I had anything to do with it?"

"I don't think he does. He cares about you, Kate. And when he looked out that window and saw J.M. Houston's arm around you, he went berserk. First Max thought that he'd lost the hotel to Houston. Then Houston practically admitted that he had someone on the inside. Then he sees you with Houston. Give him time."

"Time? I don't think so. Letting myself care about Max was a mistake. Men like Max don't mean to, but they end up hurting you. My own father was a man like Max. I knew that. I should never have let things go this far."

"Kate, if there's one thing I've learned, it's that we can't always control our lives. We're just like those fishing boats sitting out there. We plot our course, but we never know when we're going to get caught up by a storm and be set down someplace we didn't plan to be. You just have to set a new course. Now, you sit out here and enjoy the view. I'll see about something to eat."

Kate scarcely heard his last words. She sat down on one of the cushioned recliners, slipped out of her shoes, and leaned back. She was totally drained, more tired than she'd ever been before.

Her head ached and something tight seemed to be swelling behind her eyes. She closed them, trying to relax.

What had happened at the Showboat was like a bad dream, and she didn't know how to wake up. She'd told Max the truth. If Max truly cared for her, he couldn't believe that she'd betray him. But he did. Dorothea's innocent little lie had grown and grown until now even the truth didn't matter.

Kate stretched out, lifting her handbag up from the floor. Her handbag. She ran her fingers over it, circling the lemon.

"You've just about hooked him," Dorothea had joked. *"just reel him in. And if the line breaks . . ."*

Well, the line had broken all right. She'd lost Max and she was back to lemons. She had to go and fall in love, the one thing she'd sworn she'd never do. She was a fool, she had been from the beginning, sounding like some kind of Pollyanna, using lemons to make lemonade. How silly.

Kate opened the bag and took out the offending yellow fruit, looking at it hopelessly. Lemons were bitter. She sunk her teeth into the sour yellow skin. The taste reminded her of the look on Max's face when he'd seen her with Houston—bitter, bitter, bitter . . .

"Don't worry, Dorothea," Matthew Blue was saying, "I've already blocked the sale. Houston will never get the hotel. Even Max didn't know that it was my money that Red Garden used. I always have a clause written into the contract that gives me first option on any sale."

"But how come none of us knew about you being the money behind the mortgage company."

"That's what I did with my money when I sold my boats. It was my way of helping the folks I care about. I didn't want any credit, so I didn't make it public."

Kate had heard the sound of Dorothea's voice. She opened her eyes and discovered that someone —Matthew, she guessed—had thrown a cover over her. It was late. The sky was velvet black, sequined with tiny snaps of light.

"I can't understand why Max went wild like that. He loves Kate, I know he does." Dorothea's voice rose and fell, and Kate heard snatches of the conversation that rolled across her mind without invoking any emotional reaction.

". . . think so too. Perhaps that's why. After all, he was very disturbed when J.M. told him that he'd known all along just how much money the Association could come up with. Maybe all this was just too important to him, Dorothea."

"Maybe," Dorothea agreed.

"Everything he's touched has turned into gold. He's been the wonder boy, solving problems, making money, never encountering any real opposition."

"Then he falls in love with Kate. Oh, Matt, I feel so responsible. I shouldn't have played Cupid. I knew how vulnerable Max was. All this is my fault."

"Well, spouting that ridiculous story about Kate being a writer for *Maverick* magazine didn't help. When Houston turned up as the buyer, Max naturally thought Kate was the spy. It's too much of a coincidence. What made you pick that magazine?"

"I don't know why you say it was a natural reaction, Matt. If somebody told me Max was a spy, I wouldn't believe it, not in your lifetime. Besides, I just made up that *Maverick* magazine stuff on the spur of the moment. I think I heard

Lucy talking about it and it just stayed in my subconscious. You know how star-struck Lucy is."

"Well, it worked out very conveniently. You made Kate a writer for one of the most famous beefcake magazines in the world, and the owner and publisher just happened to be buying the Showboat."

"But Kate is a handyman. She really is."

"Lucy!" Kate whispered. She came stiffly to her feet. That had to be the answer.

The lemon, the talisman she'd carried for luck, dropped to the floor and rolled across the terrace into the water. *So much for luck*, Kate thought. She'd make her own from now on.

"Kate?" Dorothea cried as Kate slipped back inside. "Are you all right?"

"I am now. I think," Kate answered simply. "I've been listening to you talking, and I believe it had to be Lucy who gave the information to Houston."

"Lucy? Of course!" Matthew agreed. "It all fits. The offer was made after Lucy took off on her mysterious family business trip, wasn't it. By the time Max went to New York, Lucy had already ferreted out the figures. She took them to Houston, and he approached Red Garden, demanding an answer before Max had time to work out the problem."

"There's just one thing wrong, Matthew," Dorothea said. "I'm not sure Lucy is smart enough to pull off something like this. And I think that Max knows it."

"I don't think she came up with the idea herself. She met Houston somewhere. He was probably here scouting out the area. When Houston found out where she worked, he set it up. I doubt that Max ever took any security precautions. We've never needed any."

"But isn't that sort of thing against the law?" Kate asked, realizing that knowing the culprit wasn't going to be enough.

"Sure, but how do you prove it? I'll bet that Houston covered his tracks. You might get Lucy to confess. But it would be her word against Houston's, and without proof, we won't be able to do a thing."

"Well," Kate observed in a tired voice, "you saved the Showboat, so Max can quit worrying. Do you have the hotel courtesy car, Dorothea?"

"Yes. Why? At least, I think I told the poor fellow to wait."

"I want to go back to the hotel. I have to get my things. I can't stay there any longer."

"Where will you go, Kate?" Dorothea asked anxiously.

"I don't know. I'll have to leave my car there for the time being, until I work it out."

"I have it, Kate." Matthew slapped the table triumphantly. "You'll go to work for me."

"Doing what?"

"Well, I've been thinking about the hotel. I'm going to exercise my option as first mortgage holder and take it over. If I'm going to operate it, I'll need an assistant."

"Thank you, Matthew, but I'll tell you the same thing I told Max. I don't know anything about business. The only business class I ever took was in computers, and I . . . well, that was a disaster."

"Hell, woman, neither do I. But you know about people. You've worked with every conceivable kind of problem, and besides, the hotel already has a typist—two or three of them—and a manager. What I want is a trouble-shooter. And that's you."

Kate looked from Dorothea to Matthew and back again. "Are you serious?"

"He's serious," Dorothea assured her. "You'll be furnished with living quarters, meals, and draw a salary."

"You're sure you're not just feeling sorry for me?"

"Hell no, the one I feel sorry for is Max. He's just lost the best thing that ever happened to him."

Max. She refused to think about him or what had happened earlier. She couldn't. Of course, she really shouldn't accept Matthew's offer, but maybe she could help him out for a couple of weeks until she could decide what she was going to do. At least she knew how to handle the upkeep of a building.

"Would you consider hiring me on a temporary basis, Matthew, just until you get organized and I decide what I want to do?"

"Good idea, Kate. In the meantime, you can stay here. I'll send Dorothea back to the hotel and arrange to have your things picked up. Deal?"

"Deal," Kate agreed, "as long as you don't give me an official title. Just let me help out."

Three days later, she was helping out by going over the food selections with Matthew and Dorothea in the main dining room. Matthew had already sampled every item on the lunch menu and was definite about his decision to feature local foods only.

After a moment, Kate sensed that someone had come up behind her.

"Good afternoon."

Kate turned and gasped. The intruder was J.M. Houston.

"Mrs. Jarrett, Ms. Weston, Captain Blue."

"What are you doing here, Houston?" Matthew demanded gruffly.

"I heard that you'd decided to play innkeeper, Matthew. I was in the area and decided I'd drop in and see if you might reconsider and accept a new offer for the hotel?"

"Houston, I don't have a bouncer in this restaurant, but if I did, I'd have you thrown out."

"Look, Blue, you can't blame me for taking advantage of any information that came my way. It was just smart business."

"Business is one thing, Mr. Houston," Dorothea cut in sharply, "but your little deal hurt too many people."

"I quite agree," J.M. said smoothly. "Causing Kate grief is something I regret deeply." He leaned over, bringing his face closer to Kate as he spoke. "If there is anything I can do to help, Kate, believe me, I'll be glad to do it."

Kate thought at first that it was J.M. Houston's presence that made her skin begin to tingle. Then she identified the feeling. Max. He was there. She glanced in the mirrors behind the table and saw him standing in the doorway, clasping the lovely Lucy Pierce by the arm.

Max's eyes were narrow slashes of obsidian as he returned Kate's glare in the mirror. Kate clenched her jaw in misery as she saw the scene from Max's point of view: J.M. Houston, his hand resting possessively on her back, leaning forward intimately in conversation. Well, she wouldn't defend herself again. She'd tried that once.

She turned to Matthew. "About that job title, Matthew. I'll take one. As of right now, I'm your administrative assistant."

Kate stood, walked over to Max, and smiled. "Good afternoon, Mr. Sorrenson, Lucy."

"Kate," Max said through clenched teeth. "I've just had a little talk with Lucy. It was Lucy who slipped into my office and turned on the modem so that J.M. could access my computer through the telephone lines. She was promised a career as a Maverick centerfold for her efforts."

Lucy flinched as Max's fingertips dug into her upper arm.

"Tell her, Lucy."

"Her confession isn't necessary," Kate said quietly. "We'd already figured out the truth, Max. But thank you for coming." She'd known that she would have to face Max again sometime. But she hadn't known it would be so soon.

"Kate?" Max's voice was little more than a ragged whisper.

Go away, she wanted to scream. *Don't call my name. Don't make me want to listen to your apology. Loving hurts too much.* She had to make him understand that it was over.

Lifting her chin, Kate said, "I'm sorry, sir. As the assistant to the new owner, I should do my job properly and welcome you to the Showboat. We'd like both of you to be our guests for dinner," she added as smoothly as her unstable breathing allowed. "Oh, and Mr. Sorrenson, do have a nice day." Kate brushed past Max. It took every ounce of control, but she never looked back.

When Max Sorrenson reached the dock, Carlos Herrera was waiting. For a few weeks after his encounter with Kate at the Showboat, Max had thrown himself into solving the problems the fishermen were facing of too much competition and the diminishing supply of fish. Now he was ready to bring all the parties together. There'd been a time when he'd been certain of his actions. Now, since he'd lost Kate, he couldn't be sure of anything.

"Sorry to make you lose a good day's catch, Carlos, but what we're going to do this afternoon will make us all more money in the long run. At least I hope so."

Carlos started the engine and steered the boat out into the Gulf and down the coast. Half an hour later, there were three more boats trailing them as they crossed the bridge into St. Andrews Bay and docked.

The warehouse had been converted into a make-shift meeting hall where fishermen sat warily on packing boxes and scaling tables.

Matthew Blue ambled lazily toward the center of the group, shook hands with Max, and nodded toward a loading platform that was to serve as a stage. When Carlos hung back, Max shook his head and forced him to come along.

"Afternoon, gents," Matthew said, "I think you all know Max. He's been working on our mutual problems, and I think we should hear what he has to say."

Max stepped forward. "A year ago Matthew Blue and some others came to me as a fellow fleet owner and as someone with power outside our area. They were concerned about the declining king mackerel catch and the influx of outsiders making profits even smaller."

"Still are," someone called out. "The solution is simple," another shouted. "Yeah, keep the outsiders out."

Max waited for the din to die down. Kate had come up with the solution that day on Carlos's boat. And now it was up to him to make it work. Kate . . .

He drew his attention back to the meeting. "As you know, I've never been a fishing boat captain. But I've operated my Aunt Dorothea's ships, so I've had reason to feel the pinch. I think that I've come up with a solution."

The men quieted down and waited, expectant but suspicious.

"It all started when Matthew said that it was too bad that the fishermen didn't have the same kind of protective association as the hotel owners. And he's right. The larger fleets, such as mine and Captain Blue's, have an advantage over those of you who only have one boat. My ten tons of mackerel is a more powerful voice than your one ton."

"Yeah, yeah," the chorus agreed noisily.

"What if we could combine our catch and offer it as one? Then we could bargain as one voice."

"Yeah? But whose voice?"

Max went on to explain the concept of the cooperative venture, where the group would elect a three-man committee to act for everyone. All the catches would be pooled and sold in bulk for the best prices, with the committee taking shares proportionate to their time and investment, and the rest of the profits being divided up according to each individual's catch.

By the time they left, Carlos, Max, and a man who owned only a single boat had been selected as the first committee of the Gulfshore Fishermen's Cooperative. Max should have been elated. He should have been, but without someone to share it with, the feeling wasn't as good as he'd expected it to be. "The plan was Kate's," he explained to Matthew, "and I'd appreciate it if you would express our thanks to her."

"Why don't you tell her yourself, boy?"

• • •

Kate liked working at the Showboat with Matthew, but she decided she was too close to Max. As she dressed, she looked out her window. She could see the roof of La Casa del Sol. No matter how hard she tried, she couldn't get Max Sorrenson out of her mind.

The time had come for her to move on. But she couldn't leave without facing Max once more. He'd been wrong about her. But she'd been wrong too. She'd come to understand that any time he lost control of a situation that involved her, he responded with anger to cover his uncertainty.

She'd known, too, that he had built protective walls around himself and she'd battered them down. A grand adventure. She'd set a trap and had made herself the bait. Once he'd taken it, she hadn't known what to do.

Move on. Don't stay in one place. Keep from getting close to anybody. If she never got close, she couldn't love anybody, and she couldn't be hurt. But she'd fallen in love. Working with Matt had proved that Max had been right about one thing: She could live in the penthouse suite. She could be part of the white-collar team. But it was time to burn her bridges and get on the road. She'd find the right spot and stay there, put down roots. But first she'd talk with Max. Her mother had waited all her life for her father to return, and he hadn't been strong enough to face her. Kate wouldn't make that mistake. She brushed her hair, fastened a shell necklace around her neck, and left her room.

"Kate!" Matthew was coming in the front door as she stepped out of the elevator. "You did it. It was your idea and Max's persuasive ability that worked. The Gulfshore Fishermen's Cooperative is in business. Kate?" Matthew started toward her. "Max said to give you his thanks and to say . . . that he loves you."

Matthew closed his eyes and said a small prayer of forgiveness. He'd just been around Dorothea too long, he decided. But there came a time when the truth needed to be dressed up a little.

"He said what?"

"Give Kate my thanks."

"And . . ."

"That he loves you."

Kate might have wondered about the message if she'd stopped to think, but she didn't. She was through thinking. If the hotel driver got a ticket for speeding, she'd pay it. Right now she was going to see a man about a movie. Only this movie hadn't been made yet. And she was going to write the script.

Nine

"Kate! I'm so glad to see you." Helen Stevens was at the desk. "Are you coming back to work? I don't think the hotel can stand any more of Max as a handyman."

"Max as a handyman?"

"Yep. He's got some idea that he's been living in an ivory tower. He's given up finance and real estate for a wrench and a hammer. I'm not sure that either Joe or the hotel is going to survive."

"Joe?"

"Max ordered a uniform and apprenticed himself to Joe as a handyman. Kate, if La Casa del Sol had been dependent on Max for manual labor, we'd be underwater."

Kate smiled. So Max had decided to become a blue-collar worker. She laughed lightly, then out loud. "Oh, Helen, I think I understand. The dear, sweet man. He's working his way to me."

"He is? Well I hope that makes sense to you, because it sure doesn't make any more sense to me than the Pekingese dog that he bought yesterday. He says it's better than a bird."

"He bought a dog? Where is it?"

"He sent Mrs. Jarrett and her new companion, Polly, to the vet with it."

"And where is Max?" Kate was beginning to get an idea.

"Hold on to your hat. He's installing a new shower head in his bathroom."

"Is Joe helping him?"

"I wish. No, this is to be a surprise for Joe. I think it will be a big surprise."

"Fine. Would you help me choose a gown in the hotel dress shop and authorize me to charge it?"

"If you'll get Max out of maintenance, I'll have the hotel provide you with a whole new wardrobe."

"Just a gown and a little beauty work will do."

A short time later, Kate was examining herself in the mirror with approval.

"Oh, my goodness. When you said a gown, I thought you meant a dinner gown. You look just like Mae West."

"Great. That's what I have in mind. If Max is turning into a handyman, I'm changing into the most sophisticated woman on the Strip."

"I'd love to be a little mouse under a chair when he sees you." Helen was wide-eyed with admiration.

"By the way, Helen, would you get me a couple of lemons from the kitchen and one of those fishing rods from the guests' lost and found room?"

"Anything else?"

"Oh yes, a master key and a DO NOT DISTURB sign."

"This is getting better and better." Helen quickly brought Kate the items and walked with her to the elevator.

The two guests leaving the elevator stopped short and looked at Kate. "Are we having a party?" the woman asked eagerly.

"A private party," Kate said in her best vampy voice, "a very private party. And, Helen, when Mrs. Jarrett and Polly show up, tell them they're not invited. As a matter of fact, send them over to the Showboat and tell them to stay there until I sound the all clear."

The elevator doors slid shut, and the machine rose slowly. Kate closed her eyes and prayed. She hoped she was doing the right thing. She was taking a big chance, opening herself to humiliation and rejection. She was scared silly. By the time the door opened and she stepped out into the penthouse foyer, she was ready to turn around and ride right back down. And then she heard it, a metallic pounding, a yowl, and a splash.

Kate opened the door, slipped the DO NOT DISTURB sign on the knob, and went inside. The pounding had started up again, punctuated with expletives as Max worked at whatever it was he was doing.

Kate crept silently into the bathroom and covered her mouth to hold back a gasp. Half the shower head was gone, and water was steadily dripping from the pipe. The tile around the shower head was being systematically destroyed. Max, dressed in a maintenance uniform, was standing in the tub, his shoes submerged in water. He was not a happy camper.

"All right, Max," he was saying, "where do you go from here?"

Kate arranged herself dramatically in the doorway, the rod and reel resting against her leg, one knee bent seductively. She moistened her lips and parted them in as sensual a look as she could manage.

"Why don't you come up and see *me* when you're finished, big boy?"

Max raised his eyes, caught sight of Kate in the mirror, and blanched. He tried to whirl around, slipped in the water, and went down.

"Kate? Is that you, Kate?"

"Who else were you expecting?" She dropped the rod to the floor beside her. Next she flipped the fur and satin mules away, one at a time.

Max's eyes were like saucers as he watched her from a sitting position in the tub. Kate took one slinky step, then a second, until she was at the edge of the tub, looking down at the man who'd changed her life.

"What . . . what are you doing, Kate?" Max's voice was so hoarse that he could barely speak.

"We're making a movie, Max. But this time, I'm the director and I'm writing the script." She shook her upper body and allowed the filmy robe to fall to the floor around her feet.

"I don't understand," he began, swallowing hard.

"What do you know about lemons, Max?" She stepped into the tub. She was trembling so badly that she could barely speak.

"What do I need to know?" He'd lost his confused expression as she came face to face with him.

"Lemons are a bright, happy color. See?" She held out the lemon with one hand and dropped the strap of her nightgown off one shoulder with the other.

He took the lemon and glanced at it, never really taking his eyes from her as she dropped the other strap and allowed her gown to slide from her body. It floated into the water. She stood proudly, like a water nymph on a satin lily pad.

"But lemons are sour, Max, sour without something to add sweetness. Take a bite."

"You want me to bite into this lemon?"

"Yes, I want you to experience the bitterness of something that seems bright and warm and beautiful."

Bite the lemon? He'd have walked on coals if she'd asked him to. He parted his lips and took the lemon into his mouth, sinking his teeth deeply into the fruit.

"How does it taste, Max?"

"It's sour. But then we both knew that, didn't we?"

Kate thought he was beginning to understand her point. She reached out, took the lemon, and dropped it into the water. She took his hand and helped him to stand.

Kate felt his breath quicken as she raised her face and touched her lips to his. She tasted the bitter lemon as she used her tongue to wash away the acrid flavor until the kiss was sweet.

Kate unzipped his uniform and touched him, caressed him first with her fingertips, and then with her lips.

"Now, do you understand, bossman? I'm going to sweeten up your life. And you're going to sweeten up mine."

A huge weight was lifted off his chest. The pain he'd been holding back seemed to rip away, and Max felt an incredible release as she reached for him. He no longer tried to hold back the spasms of ecstasy that sent tears of joy down his cheeks.

"Oh, Max," Kate said, folding her arms around him, pulling his face against her breast, "don't. I love you. Everything will work out for us because we belong together. Dorothea was right, you know."

She drew back, took his face in her hands, and studied him lovingly. "We both had to grow up, break out of our prisons. Your mother left you, and you were afraid to let yourself care about anybody else. You surrounded yourself with machines and committees." Max felt the tears stop.

"But you, Kate. You managed to break away. After your mother died, you left. You've lived exactly the kind of life you wanted, a grand adventure. Why did it take me so long to see what I was doing?"

"Max, you're wrong. I didn't make my walls until after my mother died and I learned that my father had deserted us both. She loved him, but she wasn't good enough to be his wife. I never wanted that to happen to me, so I set limits."

"I don't understand." His hands tightened around Kate's waist. He didn't want to talk anymore. He wanted to bury himself inside her.

"I never stayed with one project long enough to complete the course—even my how-to classes. That implied commitment, and that's what I didn't want—until I met you."

The depth of her honesty touched him. The one time she'd dropped her walls and allowed someone inside, she'd been betrayed. Caught up in his own insecurity, he'd railed at Kate. Once he'd seen her with Houston he'd gone cold with fear, fear that he'd already lost the woman he loved.

"Kate, I know that you didn't betray me to Houston. Even before I went to the Showboat to tell you, I knew. I just didn't know how to handle opening myself up to love."

Kate laid her cheek against his chest. "I should

have taken the job you offered me, Max. I could have worked for you, but I was afraid that I wouldn't be able to give you up, and I knew that someday I'd have to go."

"But you stayed on the Carnival Strip."

"Yes. I couldn't leave."

"Can you live in the penthouse suite of La Casa del Sol, Kate?"

"My place in the sun? I'm not sure, Max. If that's what you want, I'll try. But I don't know that I'll ever be a sophisticated woman."

"That's fine. Because I don't think you really want me to be a good old boy. I've tried, Kate. Joe's tried to teach me. But I'm afraid that I'm totally inept."

"Darling, Max. I promise you that there are some areas in which you are wonderfully talented."

Kate pressed her lips to his throat. He gave out a low groan and pulled her to him, claiming her mouth with his lips. Their bodies came together, flesh pressing hungrily against flesh, creating a kaleidoscope of sensation. He cupped her bottom in his hands and lifted her, pulling his lips from her mouth and kissing her breasts with the passion of a man who'd lost all restraint.

As he captured her nipple with his lips, she felt as if she were melting. Her lower body shifted, taking the swollen evidence of his passion between her thighs. He didn't enter her, and her maddening need was driving her into such a state that she let herself say what she'd never said before.

"Max, please. Love me, Max. I want you. I love you, Max Sorrenson. I love you . . ."

When he lifted her and took her words into his mouth, he caught her legs and fastened them around his thighs. She was on fire as his hardness pulsated between their bodies.

She didn't want him against her. She wanted him inside her. Still he held back, sliding up and down, seeking, probing. And then Max stepped over the side of the tub. As he shifted her body, she guided him into her, and he gasped.

His hands were holding her so that he plunged inside her with every step he took. She squeezed herself tight, trying to hold back the tide threatening to wash over her.

"Hold on, Kate. Not yet. I can't walk and do this at the same time."

"Too late, bossman." Kate felt the first intense wave of pleasure rip through her as Max knelt on the bed. He held her against him, never allowing her to slide away as he lowered her.

Max watched her fling her head back and bite her lower lip in pure ecstasy. He'd never felt such intense joy. He'd never felt such exquisite pleasure in giving. And then the wave of heat that had taken hold of her body suddenly transferred itself to him, and all thought of prolonging the moment was swept away in a quivering release that seemed to meld their bodies together.

"Oh, Kate. I love you."

Kate sighed deeply as she felt her body climax once again.

"Did you hear me?" Max repeated as he lay across her possessively.

"I'm afraid I was too busy hearing me," Kate said softly. She'd heard him. But she didn't know how to respond. Had he just been caught up in the splendor of the moment?

"Ah, Kate. You've bewitched me. You've turned me into a weak-kneed, bald-headed Samson, and

I'm caught up in your spell. What are we going to do?"

"Max, as long as the rest of you works, we'll buy a wig."

"I think we're safe then," he said with a grin. "If not, I have the best maintenance worker in the world right here in my arms. Do you think you can take care of my problem?"

She did, and he did—two more times.

It was late afternoon when the phone beside the bed rang.

"Damn," Max said.

"I agree. I told Helen Stevens that we were not to be disturbed." Kate was lying with her head on Max's chest, her leg thrown across his lower body.

"You mean you knew when you came up here what was going to happen?"

"Yep." She put her lips on his nipple and tugged gently.

"What would you have done if I hadn't agreed?" He tightened his arms around her.

"Oh, you didn't have a choice. You'd already taken my bait. I just had to reel you in."

"You definitely do know the right kind of bait," he agreed.

The phone rang again.

"Damn! That has to be my dear aunt. Nobody else would dare to intrude. I'd better answer it, or we'll never . . ." Max gasped.

The phone rang again.

"Hello!"

Kate circled his nipple with her tongue.

Max moaned.

"Well, well, nephew. Am I interrupting anything? You sound a little strange."

"Yes! You're interrupting. What do you want?"

"Max, is everything all right, between you and Kate?"

"Kate? Ummmmmmmmmm!"

"Ummmmmmmmmm? That's all I wanted to know."

Later that evening he found Kate in the hot tub wearing the expression of a cherub.

"What are you doing in there?" he asked.

"Thinking naughty thoughts." ·

"Need any help?" He stepped down into the churning water.

"What do you have in mind?"

"A grand adventure, Kate Weston. Will you marry me?"

"You really want to marry me?"

"Yes. Tonight, tomorrow. I want to be your husband. I want to father your children. I want to help you repair your car, paint a pole, install a—"

"Marriage is enough, Max."

"You were right about me. I've been stuck up in my ivory tower, and I've missed out on so much of life. Maybe we'll do what Dorothea did and go to sea. Do you think you could live on a shrimp boat, Kate?"

"Max, I'd live anywhere with you. I've packed my sophisticated dress and my coveralls. I'm ready to move into the penthouse suite. How many children did you have in mind?"

"Let's have two or three. In fact, I'd love to have a freckle-faced, smart-talking little girl. Maybe we could get started with taking chances right now." Max caught Kate in his arms. He leaned back against the faucet, turning the handle so that the water came on full force. "This is one how-to class I'm going to enjoy."

"Wouldn't you rather move the class to the bedroom?" Kate reached behind Max, turned the knob, and watched in horror as it came off in her hand. "The handle, Max."

Max kissed her. "Forget the handle, Kate."

"But Max, we're going to have a flood. Water is going everywhere. Aren't you concerned?"

"Nope." He kissed her again. "I love the stuff, every drop of it. Let it pour. After all, I have my own handy man—eh, woman—don't I?"

"Indeed," she whispered, "you do."

"And I promise, I'll let her get around to the job—in a week or two."

THE EDITOR'S CORNER

1990. A new decade. I suspect that most of us who are involved in romance publishing will remember the 1980s as "the romance decade." During the past ten years we have seen a momentous change as Americans jumped into the romance business and developed the talent and expertise to publish short, contemporary American love stories. Previously the only romances of this type had come from British and Australian authors through the Canadian company, Harlequin Enterprises. That lonely giant, or monopoly, was first challenged in the early 1980s when Dell published Ecstasy romances under Vivien Stephens's direction; by Simon and Schuster, which established Silhouette romances (now owned by Harlequin); and by Berkley/Jove, which supported my brainchild, Second Chance at Love. After getting that line off to a fine start, I came to Bantam.

The times had grown turbulent by the middle of the decade. But an industry had been born. Editors who liked and understood romance had been found and trained. Enormous numbers of writers had been discovered and were flocking to workshops and seminars sponsored by the brand-new Romance Writers of America to acquire or polish their skills.

LOVESWEPT was launched with six romances in May 1983. And I am extremely proud of all the wonderful authors who've been with us through these seven years and who have never left the fold, no matter the inducements to do so. I'm just as proud of the LOVESWEPT staff. There's been very little turnover—Susann Brailey, Nita Taublib, and Elizabeth Barrett have been on board all along; Carrie Feron and Tom Kleh have been here a year and two years, respectively. I'm also delighted by you, our readers, who have so wholeheartedly endorsed every innovation we've dared to make—our authors publishing under their real names and including pictures and autobiographies in their books, and the Fan of the Month feature, which puts the spotlight on a person who represents many of our readers. And of course I thank you for all your kind words about the Editor's Corner.

Now, starting this new decade, we find there wasn't enough growth in the audience for romances and/or there was too much being published, so that most American publishers have left the arena. It is only big Harlequin and little LOVESWEPT. Despite our small size, we are as vigorous and hearty, excited and exuberant now as we were in the beginning. I can't wait to see what the next ten years bring. What LOVESWEPT innova-

(continued)

tions do you imagine I might be summarizing in the Editor's Corner as we head into the new *century*?

But now to turn from musings about the year 2000 to the very real pleasures of next month!

Let Iris Johansen take you on one of her most thrilling, exciting journeys to Sedikhan, read **NOTORIOUS**, LOVESWEPT #378. It didn't matter to Sabin Wyatt that the jury had acquitted gorgeous actress Mallory Thane of his stepbrother's murder. She had become his obsession. He cleverly gets her to Sedikhan and confronts her with a demand that she tell him the truth about her marriage. When she does, he refuses to believe her story. He will believe only what he can feel: primitive, consuming desire for Mallory. . . . Convinced that Mallory returns his passion, Sabin takes her in fiery and unforgettable moments. That's only the beginning of **NOTORIOUS,** which undoubtedly is going onto my list of all-time favorites from Iris. I bet you, too, will label this romance a keeper.

Here comes another of Gail Douglas's fabulous romances about the sisters, *The Dreamweavers,* whose stories never fail to enmesh me and hold me spellbound. In LOVESWEPT #379, **SOPHISTICATED LADY,** we meet the incredible jazz pianist Pete Cochrane. When he looks up from the keyboard into Lisa Sinclair's eyes, he is captivated by the exquisite honey-blonde. He begins to play Ellington's "Sophisticated Lady," and Ann is stunned by the potent appeal of this musical James Bond. These two vagabonds have a rocky road to love that we think you'll relish every step of the way.

What a delight to welcome back Jan Hudson with her LOVESWEPT #380, **ALWAYS FRIDAY.** Full of fun and laced with fire, **ALWAYS FRIDAY** introduces us to handsome executive Daniel Friday and darling Tess Cameron. From the very first, Tess knows that there's no one better to unstarch Dan's collars and teach him to cut loose from his workaholism. Dan fears he can't protect his free-spirited and sexy Tess from disappointment. It's a glorious set of problems these two confront and solve.

Next, in Peggy Webb's **VALLEY OF FIRE,** LOVESWEPT #381, you are going to meet a dangerous man. A very dangerous and exciting man. I'd be surprised if you didn't find Rick McGill, the best private investigator in Tupelo, Mississippi, the stuff that the larger-than-life Sam Spades are made of with a little Valentino thrown in. Martha Ann Riley summons all her courage to dare to play Bacall to Rick's Bogart. She wants to find her sister's gambler husband . . . and turns out to be Rick's

(continued)

perfect companion for a sizzling night in a cave, a wicked romp through Las Vegas. Wildly attracted, Martha Ann thinks Rick is the most irresistible scoundrel she's ever met . . . and the most untrustworthy! Don't miss **VALLEY OF FIRE!** It's fantastic.

Glenna McReynolds gives us her most ambitious and thrilling romance to date in LOVESWEPT #382, **DATELINE: KYDD AND RIOS.** Nobody knew more about getting into trouble than Nikki Kydd, but that talent had made her perfect at finding stories for Josh Rios, the daring photojournalist who'd built his career reporting the battles and betrayals of San Simeon's dictatorship. After three years as partners, when he could resist her no longer, he ordered Nikki back to the States—but in the warm, dark tropical night he couldn't let her go . . . without teaching the green-eyed witch her power as a woman. She'd vanished with the dawn rather than obey Josh's command to leave, but now, a year later, Nikki needs him back . . . to fulfill a desperate bargain.

What a treat you can expect from Fayrene Preston next month—the launch book of her marvelous quartet about the people who live and work in a fabulous house, SwanSea Place. Here in LOVESWEPT #383, *SwanSea Place:* **THE LEGACY,** Caitlin Deverell had been born in SwanSea, the magnificent family home on the wild, windswept coast of Maine, and now she was restoring its splendor to open it as a luxury resort. When Nico DiFrenza asked her to let him stay for a few days, caution demanded she refuse the mysterious visitor's request— but his spellbinding charm made that impossible! So begins a riveting tale full of the unique charm Fayrene can so wonderfully invent for us.

Altogether a spectacular start to the new decade with great LOVESWEPT reading.

Warm good wishes,

Carolyn Nichols

Carolyn Nichols
Editor
LOVESWEPT
Bantam Books
666 Fifth Avenue
New York, NY 10103

FAN OF THE MONTH

Hazel Parker

Twelve years ago my husband Hoke insisted that I quit my job as a data processor to open a paperback bookstore. The reason was that our book bill had become as large as our grocery bill. Today I am still in the book business, in a much larger store, still reading and selling my favorite romance novels.

My most popular authors are of course writing for what I consider to be the number one romance series—LOVESWEPT. One of the all-time favorites is Kay Hooper. Her books appeal to readers because of her sense of humor and unique characters (for instance, Pepper in **PEPPER'S WAY**). And few authors can write better books than Iris Johansen's **THE TRUST-WORTHY REDHEAD** or Fayrene Preston's **FOR THE LOVE OF SAMI.** When the three authors get together (as they did for the Delaney series), you have *dynamite.* Keep up the good work, LOVESWEPT.

THE DELANEY DYNASTY

Men and women whose loves an passions are so glorious it takes many great romance novels by three bestselling authors to tell their tempestuous stories.

THE SHAMROCK TRINITY

☐	21975	RAFE, THE MAVERICK *by Kay Hooper*	$2.95
☐	21976	YORK, THE RENEGADE *by Iris Johansen*	$2.95
☐	21977	BURKE, THE KINGPIN *by Fayrene Preston*	$2.95

THE DELANEYS OF KILLAROO

☐	21872	ADELAIDE, THE ENCHANTRESS *by Kay Hooper*	$2.75
☐	21873	MATILDA, THE ADVENTURESS *by Iris Johansen*	$2.75
☐	21874	SYDNEY, THE TEMPTRESS *by Fayrene Preston*	$2.75

THE DELANEYS: *The Untamed Years*

☐	21899	GOLDEN FLAMES *by Kay Hooper*	$3.50
☐	21898	WILD SILVER *by Iris Johansen*	$3.50
☐	21897	COPPER FIRE *by Fayrene Preston*	$3.50

Buy them at your local bookstore or use this page to order.

Bantam Books, Dept. SW7, 414 East Golf Road, Des Plaines, IL 60016

Please send me the items I have checked above. I am enclosing $_____ (please add $2.00 to cover postage and handling). Send check or money order, no cash or C.O.D.s please.

Mr/Ms _____

Address _____

City/State _____ Zip_____

Please allow four to six weeks for delivery.
Prices and availability subject to change without notice.

SW7—11/89

60 Minutes to a Better, More Beautiful You!

Now it's easier than ever to awaken your sensuality, stay slim forever—even make yourself irresistible. With Bantam's bestselling subliminal audio tapes, you're only 60 minutes away from a better, more beautiful you!

__ 45004-2	**Slim Forever**	$8.95
__ 45112-X	**Awaken Your Sensuality**	$7.95
__ 45081-6	**You're Irresistible**	$7.95
__ 45035-2	**Stop Smoking Forever**	$8.95
__ 45130-8	**Develop Your Intuition**	$7.95
__ 45022-0	**Positively Change Your Life**	$8.95
__ 45154-5	**Get What You Want**	$7.95
__ 45041-7	**Stress Free Forever**	$7.95
__ 45106-5	**Get a Good Night's Sleep**	$7.95
__ 45094-8	**Improve Your Concentration**	$7.95
__ 45172-3	**Develop A Perfect Memory**	$8.95

Bantam Books, Dept. LT, 414 East Golf Road, Des Plaines, IL 60016

Please send me the items I have checked above. I am enclosing $_____ (please add $2.00 to cover postage and handling). Send check or money order, no cash or C.O.D.s please. (Tape offer good in USA only.)

Mr/Ms _____

Address _____

City/State _____ Zip _____

LT-12/89

Please allow four to six weeks for delivery.
Prices and availability subject to change without notice.

THE LATEST IN BOOKS
AND AUDIO CASSETTES

Paperbacks

☐	27032	**FIRST BORN** Doris Mortman	$4.95
☐	27283	**BRAZEN VIRTUE** Nora Roberts	$3.95
☐	25891	**THE TWO MRS. GRENVILLES** Dominick Dunne	$4.95
☐	27891	**PEOPLE LIKE US** Dominick Dunne	$4.95
☐	27260	**WILD SWAN** Celeste De Blasis	$4.95
☐	25692	**SWAN'S CHANCE** Celeste De Blasis	$4.50
☐	26543	**ACT OF WILL** Barbara Taylor Bradford	$5.95
☐	27790	**A WOMAN OF SUBSTANCE** Barbara Taylor Bradford	$5.95

Audio

☐ **THE SHELL SEEKERS** by Rosamunde Pilcher
Performance by Lynn Redgrave
180 Mins. Double Cassette   48183-9 $14.95

☐ **THE NAKED HEART** by Jacqueline Briskin
Performance by Stockard Channing
180 Mins. Double Cassette   45169-3 $14.95

☐ **COLD SASSY TREE** by Olive Ann Burns
Performance by Richard Thomas
180 Mins. Double Cassette   45166-9 $14.95

☐ **PEOPLE LIKE US** by Dominick Dunne
Performance by Len Cariou
180 Mins. Double Cassette   45164-2 $14.95

- -

Bantam Books, Dept. FBS, 414 East Golf Road, Des Plaines, IL 60016

Please send me the items I have checked above. I am enclosing $_____
(please add $2.00 to cover postage and handling). Send check or money
order, no cash or C.O.D.s please.

Mr/Ms _____

Address _____

City/State _____ Zip _____

FBS—11/89

Please allow four to six weeks for delivery.
Prices and availability subject to change without notice.